# Past praise for Ian MacMillan's Work

for *Proud Monster*:
Ian MacMillan has ac  le in
finding the correct to: that
everyone is dehumani /riting.

for *Orbit of Darkness*:
The enormity of the Holocaust and the horrors of war leave
an indelible imprint in this extraordinary novel, composed of
kaleidoscopic fragments, equal in impact to the best of Jerzy
Kosinski.
—*Publishers Weekly*

for *Village of a Million Spirits*:
Eloquently, MacMillan shows that the truth we can absolutely
factually know...is not the whole story.
—*The New York Times Book Review*

...thoroughly convincing and ruthlessly absorbing...stands as a
testament to the proposition that a well-chosen word is worth
a thousand pictures.
—*Jerusalem Post*

for *Squid-Eye*:
Here's a book that brings you eye to eye with life in Hawai'i—
not the flowery, painted-over stuff but the real nitty gritty.
—*Honolulu Advertiser*

# Also by Ian MacMillan

## Stories

*Ullambana: Short Stories of Hawai`i*
*Squid-Eye*
*Exiles from Time: Short Stories of Hawai`i*
*Light and Power*

## Novels

*The Bone Hook*
*The Seven Orchids*
*The Braid*
*Village of a Million Spirits: A Novel of the Treblinka Uprising*
*The Red Wind*
*Orbit of Darkness*
*Proud Monster*
*Blakely's Ark*

## Nonfiction

*Paddling in Hawai`i: A Photo Essay* (text)

Our
people
Stories

Ian MacMillan

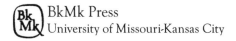

BkMk Press
University of Missouri-Kansas City

BkMk Press
University of Missouri-Kansas City
5101 Rockhill Road
Kansas City, Missouri 64110
(816) 235-2558 (voice) / (816) 235-2611 (fax)
www.umkc.edu/bkmk

Cover art: Ryan MacDonald
Book design: Susan L. Schurman
Managing editor: Ben Furnish
Assistant Managing Editor: Susan L. Schurman

BkMk Press wishes to thank: Elizabeth Gromling,
Cara LeFebvre, and Gina Padberg.
Special thanks to Karen I. Johnson.

This project is supported in part by an award from
the National Endowment for the Arts. Financial
assistance for this project has been provided by
the Missouri Arts Council, a state agency.

NATIONAL
ENDOWMENT
FOR THE ARTS
A great nation
deserves great art.

Library of Congress Cataloguing-in-Publication Data

MacMillan, Ian T.
  Our people : stories / Ian T. MacMillan.
    p. cm.
  ISBN 978-1-886157-67-5
  1. New York (State)—Fiction. 2. Farm life—New York (State)—
Fiction. 3. United States—Social life and customs—20th century–
Fiction. I. Title.

PS3563.A318955O97 2008
813'.54–dc22

                              2008023999

This book is set in Goudy Old Style, Matura MT, and Myriad.

for Susan, Julia, Laura, Rick, and Emma

## Acknowledgments

Thanks to the publications in which these stories previously appeared: *West Wind Review, Yankee, Fiction Network, Porcupine Literary Arts Journal, R.S.V.P., Green Hills Literary Lantern, Natural Bridge, Kansas Quarterly, Gettysburg Review, Potpourri,* and *Prize Stories: The O. Henry Awards.*

# The Fence

Jay McGrath estimated the time at 4:30 A.M., and slipped
out of the bedroom window onto the dew-silvered grass,
leaving the smell of urine in the room.  His two little
brothers did it once or twice a week on the six-inch bed of
dirty clothes that covered most of the room's floor.

In the barn he got the flashlight and moved quietly,
working the heavy cover off the milk can and dipping
down under the cream on top with a galvanized steel la-
dle.  He put the milk in a mayonnaise jar and then went
to the garbage can where they kept the dog food, and put
it in a paper bag he had jammed under the can.  Mike,
the old collie tied in the manger, did not bark, because Jay
had done this every night for nearly two weeks.

It was so bright out, with the immense canopy of stars
and the ashy light of dawn on the eastern horizon, that as
he walked he could easily read the blue label on the jar.
He went up the middle rut made by the front wheels of

the Farmall, seeing the shapes of the cows sitting in the pasture to his left.

The tracks angled toward the electric fence, and he looked at the single wire mounted on the white insulators nailed into the quarter round locust posts. When he got to within ten feet of the fence he stopped, and could just hear the rhythmic clicking of the junction box a hundred yards behind him.

He put the jar of milk and the dog food down, and walked to the fence. After hesitating a few seconds, he reached out and grabbed the wire with both hands, and the rhythmic pulse of the low voltage current pounded in his arms, so that his muscles and blood veins surged in a hard, thumping heartbeat. His brother Ben had showed him this a long time ago. Ben left the day he was eighteen without saying a word to anyone, and when his father came home from his work with the County Road and found out he had joined the Marines, he sat at the kitchen table for a half an hour saying, "That stupid jerk! The Navy! I tol' him a thousand times, the Navy!" But they all knew, his mother, Jay, even the little kids, that Ben hated his father enough that he would have done anything but what his father had done, join the Navy. For days after that his father would sit at the kitchen table in the morning and mutter, "Marines," and then shake his head with a strange, pained expression.

The pulsing of the electricity did something, soothed him maybe, so that after twenty seconds he found himself giggling, watching his arms surge with each pulse, and then all the stars seemed brighter. He let go one hand, and the pulse doubled in power, becoming painful, and he stared at the cows, two of them up now and looking at him. Ben had once called him over to the fence as he held it, and when Jay got to him, Ben touched him on the cheek and it stung so much that he cried while Ben stood there laughing.

Sometimes he thought the fence made him see things —when the soothing, almost hypnotic trance took over, he thought he might even see the future, and now, with both hands gripping the wire, he watched one cow approach slowly, its bag swinging, and saw what he hated seeing since it happened. Maggie, the red hound, along with six pups all lying behind the barn with their skulls caved in and his father walking away, a ball-peen hammer in one hand. Almost a year ago, and it seemed like last week. Sometimes the fence made him see the past all too clearly.

He let go. They always had too many dogs, his father had said. Now they were less another, because when the female collie-shepherd Scrap started getting fat, like a hard barrel, Jay waited as long as he could and then took her into the woods and tied her up there, so far from the house that her barking wouldn't be heard. Everyone assumed that she had run off.

He went toward the woods half running, holding the jar out in front of him so that the milk sloshed and the dog food danced in the bag. He had fooled around at the fence too long.

She was tied up on a piece of wire he had strung from one tree to another near the foundation and remains of an old house on a hardly used dirt road bordering their woods. The wire had a loop-ended leash that slid on it, giving her some space. He had hammered together a lean-to using some of the rotted siding from inside the foundation, where there were broken jars, pieces of furniture, and garden tools perforated by rust. When he approached she growled deep in her throat, and then began to whine.

"Hey Scrap," he whispered. "Hey, how you doin'?"

She was still a bloated barrel with legs. He shook dog food into a cracked yellow bowl he had found in the foundation, and then poured the milk on it. She lapped away at it, her body shaking. He went to the water bucket and checked the level, seeing the leaves and stars in the surface—half full. Then he heard swishing sounds in the blackness behind the foundation, and Scrap growled. For a moment he was rigid with fear. Then he shook it off and whispered, "Deer, it's only deer." The darkness made the woods strange—outside the perimeter of dim light, where the yellow bowl looked white and Scrap was a ghostlike specter, it was all velvet black.

On his way back he pushed himself to a half run along the fence, carrying the empty jar. The sky was getting lighter and soon it would be time to get the cows, and he had to climb back in the window before his mother got up.

It was bad, the way Ben left. Because he was the oldest he had grown up taking the biggest share of the abuse from their father. Make a mistake, you get a whack across the head, and age didn't matter. Wet the bed and you got beaten up. Ricky and Bob were now used to it. In fact the last time their father beat them for that Ricky reasoned between shots to the head and shoulders that it wasn't a bed—"Old rotten clothes!" he said. "That's all it is," and there the beating stopped.

Their father was a mean bastard and well known for it, even liked for it. Once on a Sunday when they were in the woods cutting firewood with the neighbor men, he told them that he had solved his dog problem with "the ball-peen treatment," and they all laughed, Ben along with them. But when Ben and Jay were alone loading the chunks onto the splintered planks of a flatbed truck, Ben told him that he hated all this, he hated his father and he hated the dirt and going to school smelling like a cow and hated it that day when he had to drag Maggie to the hole while Jay followed, carrying the puppies with their flattened skulls in an oily cardboard box.

Around the same time Jay knew that Scrap was going to have the puppies, he knew that Ben would be leaving. They were near the pasture, and Ben grabbed the electric fence and said, "Hey, c'mere." When Jay shook his head Ben let go and looked at him. "How tall are you?"

"Five seven, maybe eight."

"Hell, you'll be six foot 'fore you're sixteen." He looked off into the woods. "It's like—" He shook his head slowly. "It's— I mean there's somethin' I—"

"What?"

Then he said, "Nah, c'mon, let's get back."

It took Jay a full minute before he understood, and he thought, he's leaving, that's what it is. In his family people rarely spoke directly about anything important. It was usually around the edges. Sometimes during the beatings of the boys his mother would turn from the sink, look at Jay and produce a sustained shrug that said, what can I do? When the beatings got obviously too harsh she would walk into the living room and say, "Here!"

Two weeks after Ben left, when Jay had decided to take Scrap to the woods, his older married sister came over and showed his mother a post card from a Marine camp in North Carolina. Ben wrote that he would have even joined the foreign legion to avoid the Navy. He badly misspelled half of the words, so that it read, *forien legien*, and that worried Jay, because he imagined that the ridicule they had endured at school would now follow Ben all the way down there.

His father worked half a day on Saturday and it was on that day that Scrap had the puppies, five of them. At four o'clock in the morning he approached the lean-to and heard not that deep warning bark but a muffled woofing, and he went to her whispering, "Hey Scrap, how you doin'?" and could just make them out all in a row at her belly. He had the impulse to run back and tell Ben, and then remembered he was gone. He reached into the lean-to and picked one up, and there was a little liquid sucking pop of its muzzle coming loose. It was heavy, and had that rich, almost rubbery smell of puppies. He put it back and set Scrap's food out and then ran back toward the house, because dawn was coming. Twice he stopped, looked back—what if one of them crawled out? or if a predator of some sort—but it was no use worrying. Only a few weeks until school, and he'd give them away.

He thought that his plan was nearly foolproof. The pups would be five or six weeks old, and he could convince some of the boys to take them. The prospect was scary because he didn't really know how to approach kids who talked about Nintendo and VCR's, who made plans to go to each others' houses to watch video movies, whose lives seemed to him a paradise to live. But he would do it regardless of his shame, that long-standing reputation his family had. Whenever he had thought it might fade away, something would happen—in June Ricky was stopped by the nurse one morning, and she parted his hair and found a blue tick as fat as a pea attached to his scalp. Of course everyone saw that, and the word spread so fast that they became known as "the tickheads" before the end of the day. But if his plan worked, Scrap would miraculously return, having followed her instincts like those long journey dogs in the movies.

After the milking on that Saturday morning, his father went off to work. The problem was that in the afternoon he might decide to cut firewood or hunt woodchucks as he sometimes did on weekend days, and if so, he could get close enough to Scrap to hear her. But his father seemed moody, not his usual self as they worked in the hiss-chuck hiss-chuck sound of the milking machines, Jay careful not to make any mistakes. He had learned early that you couldn't make mistakes the way Ben had. There could be no spilt milk, no lost tools, nothing.

After the milking Jay ran back to the woods, to work on the lean-to so the little pups wouldn't get out. In the daytime he got a better look at them—black bleeding to tan on the bellies, and two of them spotted on the back like pintos. Their tails were short and fat, their ears soft half disks attached to their round heads.

He dug a trench across the lean-to opening and fit a weathered plank in. Then he walked out of the woods, feeling exhausted. It would be worse once they could move around, and he wondered if he should turn Scrap loose. But then she might go home. He stopped at the fence, remembering Ben and one of his jokes—he would grab it and yell, "I need a charge, I need a charge!" and shake as if he were being electrocuted.

Jay grabbed the fence, and watched his forearms pulse, the veins surging. Because he was so tired, there was a strange, soft hurricane of imagery in his mind, of Ben ridiculed for being unable to spell, of his father going to the woods with his hammer, looking for Scrap, of Jay himself sitting in class with puppies in his pockets, and no takers. He let go, sighed and went on toward the barn, the silver dome of the silo jouncing in his vision just over the grassy, cowpie speckled hill.

Saturday night he fell asleep on the living room floor while everyone watched the old television, and later shook himself out of his sleep and stumbled to his room, and much later in the night, which was still and warm, he woke up from a dream and heard something in the far distance. A series of shrill sounds, like a dog fighting. He thought, no, too far, but heard it again coming across the breezeless darkness. The kids moved, one of them making clicking sounds with his mouth. He stared wide-eyed at the darkness, and then got up.

He heard nothing more as he walked under the dome of stars carrying the milk and dog food, and he felt as if he walked in his sleep, the dark humps of cows to his left, the hedgerow to his right. When he approached the lean-to he felt something wrong, a smell maybe. The sky to the east was lightening, and he could see the spaces through the tall treetops.

She was in there nursing, and he said, "Hey Scrap, how you doin'?" He put the milk and dog food down and petted her. His fingers ran across something and she squealed a little. Then he felt her muzzle, and there were hard spines, some sharp as needles. He squinted and saw white foam dripping off her muzzle. "What's this?" he whispered. He counted the puppies—four. He reached behind her back and felt around, but couldn't find the fifth. Then in the increasing light he saw it in the corner, touched it and found it cold, the skin stiff.

Scrap squeaked again, and then he understood—a porcupine. A neighbor had a dog who died after getting into a fight with one. He concentrated, trying to see, and lifted her head. Then he slid his thumb through the foam into her mouth and opened it. There was just enough light—the inside of her mouth looked like two hairbrushes facing each other, and some of the quills ran through her tongue. He tried pulling one white spine out of the thin loose flesh of her cheek, and she squealed as it came out. It was around an inch long. He sat down in the leaves.

Pliers. If he pulled them out—but it was Sunday. In less than an hour the cows had to be in their stanchions.

"Scrap," he whispered.  He left the milk there in the jar, and ran back out of the woods and up over the hill.

He knew it was already too late to do it but he grabbed the needlenosed pliers from the box in the milkhouse and ran back up over the hill, passing the cows who were already aimed at the pasture gate and ready to be milked. Maybe his father would sleep late.  He stopped and looked down at the cluster of buildings, and whispered, "The hell with him."

She was still nursing the four puppies.  He sat down and cradled her head in his lap, and pulled one quill out of her cheek, his hand shaking so that he could hardly hold the pliers still.  The next one, in her black nose, seemed to have lodged in the bone it was stuck so hard, and she fought him as he pulled it out, leaving a little half sphere of dark blood enlarging at the spot where the quill had been.

After he pulled a number of them from her lips and tongue and then held her mouth open to get those that were buried like nails in the roof of her mouth, she stopped fighting and settled down.  There was hardly any blood.  Every minute or so he realized how late it was and began to shake, and whenever he grated the pliers against her teeth gooseflesh erupted on his arms.

He had no idea how long it took, but when he was done and nearly all of the quills were out, at least those that didn't break off at the level of their entry, he pulled the puppies off and led her out to the water bucket.  She drank, shaking, then sniffed the dog food and went back into the lean-to.  He thought that with more focus he could get the broken off ones, and decided that he would sneak back later in the day.

He had to go and face the music.  By now his father would have seen that the cows weren't in the barn, and

Jay would have to pay for that. He made his way back but before he broke over the hill he stopped and went to the fence and grabbed it, and watched his forearms pulse, trying to neutralize the dread he felt. But it was no good—it was only electricity, and he would have to face him anyway.

When he got to the barn his father and Ricky were getting them into their stanchions and he joined them, slapping rumps and throwing shut the smooth, worn slats of the stanchions. Then he went to the milkhouse to return the pliers and get the machines ready. His father caught him there.

"Where the hell were you?" he asked.

"Woods."

"Why?"

"I heard something."

He waited for the shot, relaxed and almost mesmerized with the expectation of it. But his father turned away and said, "'Heard something,' he says," and carried a machine into the barn, the cups dangling on their red rubber tubes.

Jay watched him, and thought, what the hell's the matter with him? That he didn't follow through with something so automatic as a slap to the head made him suspicious.

In a lull in the early afternoon, when his father sat in the living room with the Sunday paper, Jay slipped out of the house, got the pliers, and headed for the woods. In the glassy, windless heat of early afternoon, he stumbled along, exhausted and sapped of energy. He went once to grab the fence, but the pulsing of electricity was more irritating than anything else.

Scrap was nursing, and the dead pup was still in the back corner. Jay dug a hole with a rusted shovel head from the foundation and buried it. Then he went to check Scrap's mouth. He had gotten all but four or five, and the holes in her cheeks and tongue had closed up. He got out the pliers.

Someone was near. It was not the swishing rhythmic sound of deer. He looked up and saw his father standing thirty feet away, holding his rifle. Scrap wagged her tail and looked at him. His hands shaking, Jay reached into the lean-to and one by one took the pups out and put them in the hem of the front of his tee shirt, and drew it up so that they rested there as if in a bag. Scrap began to anxiously sniff at them. He looked at his father and said nothing.

"Well what's this?" he asked. "Why are you—"

Jay remained silent, and his father looked, seemed to almost nod, a strange, wondering expression on his face. After ten seconds of silence, he said, "Your grandparents lived here once. Long time ago."

"Are you—" Jay stopped himself.

"What's this with the fence?"

"What fence?"

He looked away again, then said, "What's with the pliers?"

"She got into it with a porcupine. She's all right."

"Lemme see 'em," he said, approaching.

Jay opened the shirt, and his father looked in, then looked away with a thoughtful scowl.

"Okay," Jay said. "Is it the ball peen treatment?"

His father shook his head, with that same pained expression he wore in the morning when he muttered, "Marines." He lifted the pinto-spotted one out and turned it over. "Male," he said.

"One died."

"One sometimes does," his father said. "These look healthy though." He looked around again, thinking, still holding the squirming pup in one hand, the rifle in the other. Then he said, "Bet that porcupine lives inside that old foundation."

"Think so?"

"Bet it does," he said. "Let's get them down to the barn." Jay looked in his shirt. "This one's a looker," his father said, holding the pinto-spotted one out.

When they were out of the woods, Scrap walking along always nose up from Jay to his father, Jay said, "It was just some fun Ben and me had. The fence I mean."

His father looked at the fence, and after a few seconds said, "You know, I wish I'd a never— I mean—" Then he gestured vaguely with the rifle, and lifted the pup up to look at him. Jay waited for him to continue but he didn't.

He shifted the pups in his shirt and said, "Look, isn't it like—I mean soldiers get leave, don't they?"

His father shook his head doubtfully. "Yeah," he said, "but what if he don't come home? I mean suppose—"

"Bet he will," Jay said.

His father seemed about to say something else, but instead shrugged his shoulders, holding the pup against his chest, and they walked the rest of the way in silence, along the single bright line of wire.

# The Potato Man

At first I couldn't figure what was wrong with her. We were standing out there looking at all those acres of hay and waving barnyard flies away from our faces, and she had this surly, pinched look on her face. She said, "Your idea's dumb. I mean it's stupid."

"Nothing else to do," I said. "Maybe we can sell it."

"For what? So we can go to Europe? California?"

She walked off toward the house. I pulled a reed of timothy out of its stalk and chewed the soft end, folding it into my mouth in half-inch sections. It tasted like it smelled, sweet, like cows' breath. I guessed that because Caroline hated everything these days, she hated the hay and my idea. She was eighteen; I was thirteen.

Sometimes my father came out of the house on his crutches to look around. He would lean on them, his body sort of limp, so that the tan crutch pads drove way up his armpits, making his shoulders look like those of a bat. He would spit, shake his head, and then pole his way back into the house.

"We can cut wood," I would say to no one. Or, "We should cut this hay now."

Our new machinery had just been repossessed, partly because of the medical bills for my father's leg, partly because of rising feed and electricity costs, partly because of a late spring rush of veterinary bills. We lost the Farmall, the baler, side rake, crusher, the new manure spreader. And the other older equipment we had sold to make down payments on the new machinery.

I made my way through the weeds and burdock bushes to look at the old stuff that my grandfather had used. There was a little Allis Chalmers tractor that was dead, its orange paint bleached almost white; there was an old hay cutter with a six-foot sickle bar fused shut by rust. It had a seat on a long leaf spring out behind the axle and the large iron wheels, and a clutch pedal for the sickle bar, and a long hand lever for raising the bar up. A long time ago I bounced on the seat for fun. There was a dump rake by the driveway, almost hidden in the tall weeds. The strangest machine was a huge hay loader, a complicated-looking gizmo of rusted metal, square linked chains, wooden slats, large iron wheels with cleats, the whole thing probably twelve or more feet high. It had old bird nests in it, and vines had just about covered it up so that it looked like a giant hand coming out of the ground with the palm facing downward at a 45-degree angle.

You just didn't leave good hay to dry up like that. But nobody really cared. My father nursed his broken leg, my mother nursed my father and watched TV, and my sister went around looking as if she had eaten something bad. Her boyfriend had left town to join the navy. Without even saying good-bye, supposedly. And then his family left for Albany.

And we were losing our place, or so I understood. We still milked the cows and kept the barn clean, but were not doing any of the summer work. My parents talked in the evenings about selling our land to the Potato Man. He was a grower who acquired land, especially with acid soil like ours. He had a lot of the old farms around—Morehouse Hill Grown Potatoes, the sign would read. Our house was in an area up high and eight miles from the town, where along the dirt roads you could see the hilled-up rows out behind empty houses and dry-rotted barns.

I figured to start with the cutter. I got a bucket of used, gritty oil from the oil shed and poured it on the axles, the sickle bar, and the clutch mechanism. Then I went to clear out the weeds and oil the dump rake. There was a crescent wrench in the bottom of the bucket.

Caroline came back out. "We're gonna eat."

"...'kay." I rubbed the crescent wrench in the weeds.

Caroline snorted. "This stuff has been out of commission for twenty years. You kidding?"

"You don't let hay dry up."

There was a thing about us up in the hills and townies. It wasn't that bad really, but I didn't want to be a townie.

"Well," Caroline said, "better get used to it."

"You're a townie," I said. "Because of whoosis—Bill."

She flushed. "Shut up. Just get off my back about that."

At night I could sometimes hear hushed, urgent-sounding conversations coming up through the black floor register in my room. I imagined that they were arguing about whether or not to sell out to the Potato Man. One time I went down the stairs, figuring on letting them have my opinion. This time it was my mother and sister. When I walked into the kitchen in my pajamas, they both looked at me as if I had come from Jupiter.

"You're talking about the house," I said.

"We're talking about soap operas," my sister said. She was smoking a cigarette.

"You don't smoke," I said.

She looked thoughtfully at the cigarette. "No," she said, "but then wait." Her face took on a look of fake surprise. "Apparently I do. Ma, look at this."

My mother sighed.

I tried cranking up the Allis, and the motor turned over, which surprised me a little because I thought it would be frozen inside. Next it was the spark plugs. The ones it had were old, the white porcelain stained by rust. When I got the first one out, using a long screwdriver and a plug socket, I found that the threads were shiny and even a little oily.

"Sand the gap," my father said. "They should be good." He was draped on his crutches. "It's the wiring you gotta check. The thing there that makes the spark."

"How's your leg?"

"Not bad. Itches like hell though."

He helped me with the wiring. He didn't say anything about all the oily machines and all the weeds and grass stamped down around them. After he left, I got gas from the oil shed and drained the little bit of old gas from the tank. It had turned and smelled like stale soap.

I thought I was going to pull every muscle in my trunk throwing the crank and was cursing with every breath before the motor coughed once and sent a puff of bluish, oily smoke out the muffler pipe. After that it was another half hour of cranking, and the engine ran, hitting on three cylinders out of four—da-da-da-sst, da-da-da-sst. I throttled it up a little, but the fourth cylinder wouldn't work.

First it was the mower. After slowly pulling the tractor away from the weeds, feeling the stiffness in the steering and the clutch, I lurched it around and backed it up to the mower tongue. There was no pin for the drawbar hitch, so I went to the house to ask my father where it was.

"Why's she so goddamned obstinate?" I heard him say.

I stopped in the woodshed.

"She says he's coming back," my mother said. "She says that ten times a day."

When I understood it, I tiptoed back out and went to the barn. "So you're gonna be an uncle," I whispered. "So that's why he left." I remembered seeing them in his car at night when he brought her home, from my bedroom window. They'd spend a long time before she came in. If anything, I was ashamed by it because the people in town would know. Then I saw the shaft of dusty light coming down through the haymow vent. It was 3:30 and time to get the cows.

After the milking we would usually watch TV, but this night I went back to try the mower out. I used a large screwdriver with a yellow plastic handle for a pin. When I dragged the mower forward, the wheels skidded for about ten feet and then turned. I thought of going to get Caroline to sit on the mower, but figured she shouldn't be doing that, so I set the tractor and mower up at the beginning of the field, lowered the bar, and undid the clutch. Again the wheels wouldn't turn. The three-inch serrated teeth were lined up on a thin bar, so I took the screwdriver pin out and tapped along on the rivets of the teeth to loosen the bar. It was already almost dark—a yellow glow on one horizon, stars and moon coming out on the other. I put the pin back and jerked the mower ahead three more times, and the bar suddenly clattered loose. The hay fell down behind it.

Because no one was on the seat, I had to let the sickle bar bounce on the rocks and chuck holes. The mower made a loud rat-a-tat sound above the sound of the three-cylinder engine.

I asked my father about the dump rake.

"Is this getting out of hand?" he asked my mother. She shrugged. "Well, all right," he said. "You can gather up a lot and make piles of it, or you can make windrows."

"I want windrows."

"The show's back on," my mother said, and left the kitchen.

"You'll need someone to sit on the rake seat—you go across and pull the trip every fifteen feet or so, and then let the teeth down again, go fifteen feet—see what I mean?"

So I asked my sister the next day while we milked. There were three milking machines all going hiss-chuck, hiss-chuck, and the milk raced along the flyspecked clear plastic pipes to the milkhouse tank.

She draped the upper part of her body over a Holstein and looked at me. "You know," she said.

I shrugged. "Don't mean no nevermind to me." I looked away, feeling a little embarrassed that she would bring it up, and said, "I just need somebody to sit on the rake."

"You're ashamed."

"No. I just want to make sure that when it's cut somebody'll sit on the rake is all I was getting at."

"All right," she said. "Let me know when."

The mower broke when I had four-fifths of the field cut, with about four acres left. The bar the teeth were riveted on, snapped in the middle. I went to the house to ask my father about the scythes.

"Count me out," Caroline said.

My father told me that if I wanted some big shoulders and some big blisters, sure, go ahead. But sharpen them first.

The trick to using a scythe is to cut only a foot of hay or less with each stroke. Then you get into a kind of rhythm in the swing. When you drive the point into the dirt, the handles are torn from your grip and the long, curved neck bangs your hip or knee. I scythed the rest of the field, got dime-sized blisters on the palms of my hands, but the repetition of it drove all the junk from my mind. And I started working on this expectation that doing this would turn the tide, the way it happens in movies.

I sat on the rake because being a driver, Caroline could work the clutch better. The dump rake is a simpler machine, and it worked right away. While we gradually made the rows longer, each by the width of the rake each crossing, I watched her, thinking of her and her jerk boyfriend, Bill. She acted as if nothing was wrong and didn't have that surly expression anymore. It was because she had decided to keep the baby. When she stopped the tractor and got off to stretch, I waited a second in the peculiar silence and said, "Do you want to live in town? I mean with—"

She looked at me. "I get it. We stay here and nobody finds out, right? You think I care about people in town?"

"Don't you?"

"Look, the Potato Man's gonna get all this. You're wasting your time. This isn't gonna get you anywhere."

"You think I'm doin' this because I'm worried about him? What is he anyway? A potato with legs?" I bounced on the rake seat a little. "I'm doin' this for fun, for the pure hell of it. Besides, you're keeping that—the—" I looked down at her stomach, and she laughed loud, as if I had told a good joke.

"I know what I'm doing," she said, and climbed back up on the tractor. "Hey, crank it up, willya?"

At dinner it was all looks, easy to read. Caroline was flip, acted hungry. My mother was sad and sort of perplexed. My father ate in jerks, thumping his cast on the floor—he shot looks at them as if they had conspired against him.

"I'm gettin' the hay loader out tomorrow," I said.

"It'll never work," my father said. "It's a heap of trash—scrap metal."

"I oiled it."

"Oh," he said, "well, in that case—" Then he clicked his tongue and went on eating in jerks.

After a minute my mother said, "It's time to think straight. These are modern times."

"Ma," Caroline said, leaning over close to her. "Ma, I went to school. I know what year it is."

"Coulda fooled me," my father said.

After another silence I said, "What's all this about the Potato Man?" Nobody answered.

The hay loader. The complexity of the machine made it seem impossible. The way it worked was that it moved forward while a drum-shaped cage bristling with rods turned in the opposite direction, lifting the hay on the slats on a kind of conveyor mechanism five or six feet wide, all the way up to where it would go level for three feet and then drop the hay onto a wagon bed. I tried the lever that put it in gear, and the mechanism moved with a gritty squeaking. One slat was broken way up toward the top, so I climbed up the conveyor, on the side so that I wouldn't break the other slats. It was loose, like a wide rope ladder. I did the repair with a flat, foot-long piece of iron with holes in it, using one of those Craftsman push screwdrivers and a little drill bit where the screwdriver bit went. I took the nuts and bolts off my old Radio Flyer wagon in the barn. The blisters on my hands were so sore it took a half an hour, with me all pretzeled up on the conveyor with those steel rods sticking out.

Caroline came out and down to the loader. "Dad said to get off there before you break your neck."

"I'm fixing the slat."

"He's talking to the cow man.  On the phone I mean."

"So?"

"Just thought you oughta know."  She looked at the house.  "I don't like it either.  Next it's the Potato Man."

"Can you help me with this?  I mean when it's ready?"

"Sure. You gonna watch the movie tonight?  It's North By Northwest.  Cary Grant."

"...'zat where he climbs on Lincoln's nose?  Sure."

We had another dinner with the thumping of the cast and significant looks.  I kept my mouth shut.  Later while Caroline and I waited in the living room for the movie, I heard my father in the kitchen say that the man would make his offer tomorrow.  Then he thumped the floor with his cast.

"What offer?" I asked Caroline.

"Either from the potato with legs or the other guy, the one with the spotted hide and horns.  Who knows?"

"What do they call the mountain Cary Grant climbs on?"

"Rushmore?"

I got up.  "I'm gonna drag the loader out."  She shrugged.

The tractor started on the first crank, but still hit on only three cylinders.  When I pulled the loader out, I could hear the snapping of the vines and the groaning sound of the wheels, but since it was not in gear, it came out easily.  I parked it at the beginning of the first wind-row and drove back to the barn to get the hay wagon and a pitchfork.  The wagon had rubber tires and was easy to hook up behind the loader. When I had the tractor set up in front of the hay loader, Caroline came out.

"It looks like a little train," she said above the idle of the tractor. "Did you ask Dad if you could do this?"

"No. You wanna drive the tractor?"

"It's almost dark."

"So?"

She got up on the tractor, and I put the loader in gear.

"It won't work," she called to me. "It looks like something a monkey built with an erector set."

"Just pull it."

The wheels skidded and she stopped. She backed up, and the wheels turned about an eighth of a turn. Then she lurched forward, and when the loader was supposed to skid again, there was what sounded like an explosion, and then there was this terrible clanking racket as the huge conveyor chain began to turn. It was like fifty people banging garbage cans, and inside that was the sharp, machine gun rat-a-tat of the chain banging around the huge gears. I jumped up on the wagon, and the hay started coming over the top. She slowed down again, and I picked up the pitchfork and leaned out over the side. "Second gear!"

When she hit the throttle again, the huge wads of hay came down on my head. It was all so loud that I felt myself pulling into it, almost as if it were a deep silence, and started pushing the hay toward the corners of the wagon bed. Caroline came out with a savage whooping sound.

We went up one row and down another back to the house. By then the wagon was one-third full. She put the throttle back to an idle and got off.

"My God," she said. "It was like three freight trains. What an invention!"

"This is fifty years ago, a hundred," I said.

"Well, it's dark," she said. She looked at the house, thinking, and then laughed again. "You know, I'm not stupid. He isn't coming back. Bill, I mean."

"Well, you never know," I said. "I mean, how would you know for sure?"

She looked at me and smiled. "You wanna keep going? It's my turn on the wagon."

"You think you should, what with the—you know...."

"You're sweet," she said, jumping up on the wagon bed. "But I'm not made of glass. What happens next?"

"The hook up under the ceiling of the barn, on that heavy rope? We drop that with a kind of trigger, I think. It has hinged blades that take a big wad of hay—then the pulley lifts it up and runs it to the haymow where we pull the trigger again. Bombs away."

"Is that what that is," she said, half question and half statement. "All I remember is that we were never allowed to play with the ropes. C'mon, let's go. Make it go fast."

When I got up on the tractor, I saw my father standing there by the back door watching. I waved, and he shook his head. Then he gestured to me, I think to stop, but I looked away quickly and lurched forward, making Caroline scream briefly. Then I could hear her laughing, probably because of all the hay coming down on her. I didn't look back, because I was sure I was disobeying my father. I gritted my teeth and cringed and upped the throttle. Caroline yelled something to me and came out with another whooping sound, which was nearly drowned out by the tremendous noise of the hay loader. It was then that I was able to feel right for the first time in a while—we were making noise for the sake of making noise. It was true that we would have to watch the obedient, grandmotherly cows walking in twos up into the trucks, we would have to stare out the window at the Potato Man doing measuring and soil testing out behind the house and across the dirt road, we would even become townies, and Caroline would gradually stop watching for the mailman, but this one night we put ourselves inside the cover of that noise—it was as if the resurrection of all this machinery wasn't a way of getting somewhere, it was the somewhere itself.

After a while my father moved the car so that he could shine the headlights out over the hayfield, right at us. The two blinding shafts meant come in, stop the nonsense. At the end of the next row near the house, when the wagon was nearly full, he stopped us. Caroline slid off the wagon bed and whispered, "The game's up. We're busted." Then she giggled.

We stood there, almost as if we were standing at attention. He stood up straight on the crutches. "I'll have to draw the line here," he said. "The hook in the barn is not a toy. Back the wagon inside, and let me show you how it works first. And it's dangerous to work in the dark. Just move the car when you need to, and don't let the battery run down."

# Our People

Pearson watched the snow tumble off his knees as he plowed along, and felt it squeak as it packed under his boot soles. His daughter, who had talked him into this, was close behind, her march easier because he broke a path for her. Even in the darkness the moonlight reflecting off the snow was bright enough to make him squint, and the sky seemed to have three times as many stars as usual, or possible. He wouldn't need the flashlight. "Why didn't you just knock on the door?" he said. She didn't say anything, and they kept walking.

"I never go to his house," she said finally.

Pearson stopped and turned, looking at her through the vapor of his breath. "Then he's down in Albany with his old man," he said, controlling his temper, and added, "who is, as I said, no friend of mine."

"Far as I know," she said, "he never goes down there. It's four days now I haven't seen him."

"How is it you go over so often and never go to his house?"

"I don't know," she said. "Mostly I look for fossils and stuff. Arrowheads."

Pearson groaned. He didn't believe her. "Well, you don't know much," he said. "I don't either."

"I—we look for—"

"Okay, I know, fossils, arrowheads, diamonds."

"Well, diamonds are down in the mid-Adirondacks. The Canadian glaciers passed by us, twenty thousand years ago. The Hudson Valley—"

"Ah," he said, "well. Twenty thousand years." He turned and looked ahead. "That's different."

The moon made a round, phosphorescent halo on the snow in front of him, with a peculiar spectral eye in the middle, and when he moved ahead again, it moved with him, glittering along the surface. "You realize this snow isn't broken because they take their wood out the other way."

"The snow isn't broken on the other side either," she said.

Pearson grunted and trudged on, thinking, the hell with it, let's just get this over with.

It was back there in September, maybe earlier, when his daughter had walked out the front door, leaving Pearson in a cloud of perfume, standing there staring at the browned cotton stapled to the screen. She got on her bicycle and went up the road, not down. "What the hell's going on?" Pearson asked his wife. "Where's she going?"

And Eileen said, "Out, I guess."

"Don't get secret," he said. "She don't need perfume for rocks."

She turned from the sink and rubbed her hands on the gray spots on her apron. "Okay, she's going out to see a boy." He kept looking at her, his arms folded. "Okay, it's the Colombo boy."

He felt a quick boilover of anger and suspicion, sniffing at the vague remnant of the perfume. But it was late morning and he had to get to work in the woods.

A month later his daughter approached him and asked if Matt Colombo could come for dinner. He should have put a stop to it the first day. He told her he'd think on it. Later he told Eileen the kid was a goddamned Brooklyn greaser and he didn't want him in the house.

She laughed and said, "He's got light brown hair, almost blond. Besides, the Colombos have been here over twenty years."

That was just the problem. Colombo came up from Brooklyn, an early retiree from the docks and went right into the wood business—pulp, stovewood, some logs. He was so enthusiastic about his new profession that he worked his way right into a section of Pearson's woods. Pearson had followed the scream of new McCulloch chainsaws and caught him and a couple of his older sons making pulp out of five-inch saplings. He tried to tell him, wait till they're bigger, cut on your own property.

"I'm on my own proppity," Colombo said.

"No you're not—you left it back a hundred yards, the stone fence by the little brook."

"I din' see no brook." His two sons talked to each other in whispers, aware that they were witnessing some sort of dispute.

Colombo suggested a "siveyih." Pearson told him a surveyor's fee would put them both out of business. The problem was never resolved. To Pearson, Colombo was an invader. It was more than a couple acres of woods, too. The Colombos were not local people.

And now, all this time later, with Mrs. Colombo dead

and the older boys gone, it was the Brooklyn Dodger's youngest kid. And the part of it that bothered Pearson was that his daughter, the last child of four, had grown up to become, at sixteen, a kind of wonder. He could not figure it out—his other children were normal, almost plain, and had gone off to lives any parent could understand. Nora, the last one, was the product of some lottery ticket genetic accident—tall and beautiful and physically almost overendowed, with dark, sultry eyes, she was also sullen and introverted. And she had a mysterious and unlikely obsession. For years she had collected arrowheads, fossils, crystals, but now her hobby had become a scientific mania. Her room was a claustrophobic combination of a museum and a library, and she spent all her summer babysitting money on books about geology, anthropology, and obscure subjects like plate tectonics. She probably knew more about the anthropological and geological history of the area than anyone within fifty miles. Usually when he walked past her open door, she would be staring at some book or lump of rock, mesmerized in a kind of scientific trance.

The strange combination of Nora's exaggerations perplexed Pearson, and when she doused herself with perfume and went out the door with that secret, unsmiling, determined look, he was scared. It was no wonder she had caught the eye of Matt Colombo, and what made it worse was that he had never seen the boy up close.

So he said, "All right. I want to meet this kid."

Nora stared at him a moment, and then, with absolutely no expression on her face, said, "Tomorrow?"

"I won't be back from the woods until five, five-thirty. Make it six-thirty, something like that."

The boy was seventeen, tall and skinny and kind of pitiful. He wore faded, threadbare Levis and a badly worn plaid shirt. Half of Pearson's fears evaporated when the boy sheepishly offered a bony hand and said, "Nice to meet you." He had no accent, and his hand was like a limp fish. Pearson shook it, feeling bones slide into a round bundle, and said, "Well, siddown, how's your father?"

The boy looked at Nora. "Uh, okay," he said. "Works down to Albany a lot now. I do the wood. I put it on the dock down to Hartwick."

"Long way," Pearson said. "Could use ours some-time." Actually he couldn't. Pearson's loading dock was small and rickety, and every time he unleashed the cords of pulpwood down it and onto the stake-truck beds, he held his breath, praying for it to hold one more time.

As they went on talking, Pearson was aware that Nora was staring at him, not at Matt Colombo.

The ground-beef patties were shaped like T-bones, a trick Eileen had made a habit years back. Matt Colombo didn't seem to notice. When he had his plate full, he set to eating with a kind of furious concentration, mixed with restraint, as if he knew manners but couldn't make himself use them more than about 30 percent. When the beef patty was gone Pearson said, "You don't go to our school—do you go to the other one? I know the district line is here somewheres—"

"I quit," he said. Then he blushed, and his ears turned red. "Last year. Too much to do."

"Wonder if you shoulda done that," Pearson said.

And the boy drew himself up, as if he were preparing to lift something, and said, "Well, I'm gonna be eighteen soon. I was thinkin' of growin' Christmas trees."

"Well, that's good money. What's your father say?"

He looked away for a moment, and shrugged.

They went on eating. The boy was making his way through the mashed potatoes and stopped, put his fork down, and sat up straight. His face seemed to have been drained of blood.

"Can I be excused?" he asked.

"Sure, what's wrong?" Pearson asked.

The boy got up and went out the back door. Nora looked at Eileen, who whispered, "What's wrong?" Nora stared at her plate, as if the answer might be there. Pearson got up and went to the window. The boy was out there standing in the dying light, and seemed to be shaking. When he turned around and looked toward the dirt road, Pearson could see that his face was contorted with pain, and he was breathing rapidly. Pearson left the window and sat down again, and looked once at Eileen, shaking his head.

The boy came back in and sat down.

"Sorry," he said.

"Is something wrong?" Eileen asked.

"I— No. Nothin's wrong."

Later, after the boy had gone and Nora was off to bed, Pearson said, "He's got a screw loose."

"I think he's all right," Eileen said. "My instincts go that way anyway. What did you see outside?"

"I don't know," Pearson said.

"Well, I think he should eat more at least," she said. "I think we ought to invite him back."

Pearson thought, no. The next day too, whenever it invaded his mind. No. He was in the barn in late morning filing the chain on a saw determined to ride to the right, when Nora came in. "Hang on," he said. "I gotta get the pressure just right or it'll try to go the other way."

When he had finished, she said, "You don't like him." The expression on her face and in her dark, beautiful eyes was like the statement—direct, scientifically objective.

"Well," he said, "I don't think he shoulda quit school."

"But you don't like him."

"He's not our—well, people. He's not our people."

"Why not?"

Pearson felt a rush of fatalistic acceptance. He knew what it was. People or deer or woodchucks—nature would pair them up no matter what he did. In country as remote as this, rolling mountains bristling with trees and only occasionally interrupted by civilization, which came in strips called roads and bleak, brush strewn clearings called farms, they paired up because they didn't have much choice. It was Pearson's bad luck that she was batting her eyes at a kid like Matt Colombo. "Look," he said, "I—you don't know anything about the world yet. Why—" He stopped and flapped his hands in the air.

"Can I invite him back?"

He sighed and went back to the saw. He didn't have the heart to tell her the boy was a loser, a waste of time. "Sure," he said.

So the kid came over twice more. The only thing that would make him talk was the chance to say more about how the world would change when he was eighteen. And then, of course, there were the Christmas trees. He continued to look away or shrug whenever his father was mentioned. His father who was always down in Albany. The more Pearson looked at Matt Colombo, the more he felt his earlier fears confirmed—the boy had something in his face, a dogged, moody, almost animal persistence, very much like Nora. They were perfect for each other. He became convinced that they were up to the obvious. Eileen laughed it off. "Let them alone!" she said. "They're kids—they like each other."

"So what do they do five hours a day?"

"Stop it! He's shy. He's young, like Nora. Besides, five hours is an exaggeration."

He didn't like what he heard from Tim Pickford down at the general store either. Tim wiped his hands on a bloodstained apron and said, "Tony Colombo? I ain't seen the old guy in months. Got a bill long's my arm here too. And that kid, somebody saw him draggin' a deer across the road a couple weeks ago. Got a little jump on the season."

So, a poacher too. Not that that was so uncommon. But anybody who spent all his time working down in Albany should be able to pay his bills and didn't need venison out of season.

The last time Pearson had seen the kid was in November, just before the heavy snow started coming down. He saw him from a distance, loading pulpwood on a hay wagon hitched to an old Massey-Harris tractor. Then he watched the boy try to cut down an angular maple. He put the wedge into the wrong side of the trunk so that the saw pinched. The tree twisted, snapped at the base, and fell. The boy scrambled out of the way just in time. Pearson felt his scalp prickle and his heart thump, realizing that the kid could have been killed. He went back to the tractor to look for wood someplace else.

And walking in the snow, watching it tumble off his knees, Pearson began wondering if some tree he tried to knock down the wrong way had finally nailed him.

The Colombos' house was dark, and Nora had been right—the snow was not broken on the other side of the driveway. Pearson stopped and studied the house. "So nobody's home," he said.

Nora stared at him and said nothing. "Okay," Pearson said, and made his way into the drive. The tractor stood outside, the body capped with a huge mushroom of snow. Beyond that was the old man's truck. "Okay, here goes," he said. He got up on the porch and knocked on the storm door. Nothing. He opened the storm door and knocked on the one inside, and waited. Then he snorted, feeling strange about the intrusion. He pulled out his flashlight and poked it into the little window. The kitchen was almost bare, only a table and two chairs, the huge black woodstove, a rust-stained sink. He was about to pull the light away when he saw something glint on the table. Then he saw a black stain, and what looked like a lot of black disks on the wooden floor.

"Something's wrong," he said.

The door was open. The black stain on the table was reddish, and in the center of it, joined by little glittering filaments of ice, was an open pair of pliers and a huge, bloody tooth, with four long roots and a crater the size of a pencil eraser in the center. "My God," he said. "Where's—" The temperature in the house was the same as outside. "Get the light."

Nora found a switch by the door, but there was no electricity. "I want to go home," she whispered.

"He—the old man must've tried to take—" Then he remembered. The boy had been eating hot mashed potatoes when he got up and left. It was a bad tooth. "The old man must've taken him to the—" No, the truck was outside.

He made his way down the hall. The boy was wrapped in a sleeping bag on the couch. When he looked up he squinted at the light. His jaw was badly swollen on one side, and Pearson could smell sickness in the heat that wafted up from him. "It's us," he said. "Nora's here."

"Wha's matter?"

"Why the hell did you let your father do it?"

"He din' pull it out," the boy said. "I did."

Pearson reached out to put his hand on the boy's forehead, and he recoiled as if about to be hit. Because of the cold the contrast was so great that at first Pearson thought his hand had been scalded. "You've got a fever."

"I'll be all right. ...'m fine."

Pearson aimed the light at the white ceiling, and the room was bathed in a dull glow. Potato chip bags and soda cans were strewn around, and off by the TV was a dismantled chainsaw sitting on a dark oil stain on the rug. On a table by the couch Pearson saw piles of magazines and what looked like pamphlets. He squinted at them—they were Department of Agriculture publications on soil, forest management, Christmas tree growing.

"C'mon," Pearson said. "I'm takin' you to a doctor. When did you take the tooth out?"

"Day before yesterday."

"And your father. Where the hell is he? I mean for God's sake. Where's your phone?"

"It doesn't work."

The boy stood up, teetered a little, and then went past Pearson toward the kitchen. Pearson followed, and found him poking a jack handle through the ice in a galvanized bucket. "Pipes froze?"

"Yeah," he said. He saw Nora standing on the porch and nodded to her. "Pump uses electricity," he said, turning back to Pearson. Then he stopped, dropped his shoulders, and said, "Oh boy. Oh boy."

"Your father ran off, right? Took off?"

"No." Pearson looked at the boy's face. Then it began to dawn on him.

"Where is he?"

"I buried him out back. That little pine grove."

"When?"

He dipped water from the bucket with a coffee cup, and said, "He died August twenty-fifth. He knew it was gonna happen."

Pearson stared at him, counting months in his mind, and said, "C'mon." Then they were walking, Pearson in front, Nora and the boy behind. From time to time she broke the silence by asking the simpler questions. "How do you feel now?" "Fine." And, "Did it hurt when you pulled it out?" "No, it was okay. It was fine."

During the walk Pearson was assaulted by a vision of Colombo knowing he was dying. Looking at the kid from—what? His bed? Pearson put himself in the man's place, imagining being faced with leaving someone like Nora behind.

Back at his own house, he installed Nora and the boy in the truck. After that it was the drive to town. A loose tire chain rapped the inside of the front fender all the way. In the annoying din of the sound, Pearson realized that a situation he had nothing to do with had bored its way into his life, and he didn't like the feeling.

Doctor Eldredge was impressed by the boy's stupidity. As he held up a hypodermic syringe that looked more appropriate for a horse, a gruesome device with three silver loops, two for the fingers and one for the thumb, he lectured the boy about tetanus, meningitis, about how an infection like this can kill you in twelve hours.

"How old are you anyway?" Eldredge asked.

"Eighteen. Almost."

"His birthday's tomorrow," Nora said.

"He'll stay here tonight," Eldredge told Pearson. "I want to watch this." Then he cleared his throat, and his expression told them to step outside. "Okay," he said to the boy, "lemme see some hip, if you got any."

Nora cried part of the way home. Once she shouted over the rapping chain, "He was alone! He pulled his tooth out!"

He explained the whole thing to Eileen. The story fit well into the catalog of lore of the region, events resulting from the memorable eccentricities of people long dead.

Later he passed Nora's room and saw her sitting at her desk, locked in her studious trance, and there with crystals and fan-shaped fossils and open books sat the tooth, like a little table on its four roots. She looked up at him with a strange, sort of noncommunicative objectivity, which made him vaguely uneasy. He nodded once and went on down the hall, and then stopped. "Hey, it wasn't me that pulled the tooth out," he whispered.

Then he thought again of Colombo lying in his bed knowing he was going to die and watching the boy pass by the door. Pearson could not remove the image from his mind.

Late the next morning Pearson saw the boy walking past the house. He went to the porch and called, "Hey, you could've phoned. It's five miles."

And the boy said, "...'sokay. No problem."

Pearson went out to the driveway. "C'mon, have some lunch." The boy looked up the road, shrugged, and came up the driveway.

"Can't eat," he said.

"Not venison anyway."

The boy laughed. "I ate all of that I could," he said. "The rest turned after the lights went out."

When they were all sitting around the kitchen table, Matt Colombo talked a little. Before his father's heart finally gave out, he had told Matt that he didn't know what to do about the "arrangements." He was afraid somebody'd try to take the place, Matt being underage and the other boys off to who knows where.

"They're gonna have a hearing," the boy said. "I talked to a state policeman this morning."

"What about relatives?" Pearson asked. "Brooklyn."

The kid stared at him, and said, "I don't know anything about that."

"Why didn't you tell somebody?" Eileen asked.

"I was scared, sorta. We didn't know what would happen. We didn't know anybody. I dug the hole six feet, like they say."

Pearson shook his head. Then he sighed and sat up straighter in his chair. "Look, I'll say this once. What you did I can't see too many people being able to do. Which means you want something pretty bad. What is it you want?"

"I don't know," Matt said. "Only I want it here, not someplace else. I was born here."

"Well, I see that," Pearson said. "So maybe we can help you. I saw you knock a tree down a while back and the only mystery to me is that you're still alive." Eileen lowered her eyebrows at him, and Nora stared. "Well?" he said. "So I'm saying he cuts with me on our place and I cut with him on his." Then he shrugged. "It's an idea. We can speak up for you with the state police too," he said to the boy.

He was aware of Nora staring at him, and for some reason he became annoyed. Then he realized that she had that fixedly inquisitive look he thought of as the scientific trance. He felt his face becoming warm. "Well?" he said to her. "What?"

"Look at him," Nora said to Eileen. "His face is all red."

# The Ash Grove

Even though my father was dying and knew it, he wouldn't cut the ash grove. We all knew he was dying but we didn't talk about it. We looked at him, my younger brothers and I, then at each other, at my mother, but no one talked about it. The boys were eleven and thirteen, and I don't know how much they really understood about it, or felt it.

Up in the barn there is a place at the back where part of the wall is gone and it opens out to a maple tree and dusty burdock bushes. I go there in the afternoon to stand at the hole when the sun slants in over the burdocks and through the maple leaves so that they are a bright yellow green, and I feel space around me and a kind of sweeping hush, a strange pause. That is where I understand it most. Would the absolute vacuum of nothingness be bad if nothing of you could be aware of it? But I hated thinking of him anticipating the nothingness.

One day we were in the ash grove. He had just finished measuring out board feet on four hard maple logs, good wood that brings good money, and he brushed sawdust from his old work jeans and said, "I know what you boys do at school. Marijuana."

"Some do," I said, and he gave me a suspicious squint.

"Could you get me some of that? Figured I'd try it."

"I could try."

"You'll get it. You know how to do that I figure."

That was a lot of talk for him. You wouldn't have known he was dying but for the boniness and the out of whack stubble on his face and the eyes which seemed bigger. Like he had been bled of whatever makes us look healthy, a layer of natural fat maybe. He got a barium test and they saw what they called a widening of the duodenal loop indicating that something was growing there and then they found the cancer in the pancreas and I looked at a picture of that in a medical book at the school library and saw that little organ and read how there are all sorts of new procedures. I tried to broach the subject in the woods but he said that he didn't want to see anything shiny ever again in his life. That was all he said.

It was fall and cool. At school we have our football games Friday nights, and that was where I would get the marijuana. Town boys play football. Farm boys don't because it takes too much time. Cows got to be milked and all that, and with us wood has to be cut—logs, pulp. One of the best woods is ash because the trees grow tall and the logs just don't thin out way up high. They're straight and tall and if they're two feet through at the bottom they're sixteen inches through thirty or forty feet up. When the sun comes down through the ash grove it slants in dusty columns making the trees look taller, almost like something from a dream, sounds like it too because of the hush, the strange silence coupled with the height of those trees, thirty-five, forty of them, and I said, we should cut them because it would be a lot of money, and it would be good for whatyoucall, and I didn't say medicine, because it was something we don't talk about. And he said, no, let's leave it for now.

So we didn't talk about his not cutting the ash grove. It was too obvious to talk about, like his dying was. How many times I did the math, thirty-five or forty trees, such and such a thickness and height, multiplied by the board feet and the money per thousand—every time it came to ten or twelve thousand or maybe fifteen if I was being stupid in the optimism of my calculating. But he would not cut the ash grove. I said to myself I sure would. If it was mine I'd cut it and buy a truck.

I got a ziplock baggie of marijuana from Buddy Case. He said never mind about the money, because everybody knew my father was dying. Even those football players out there knew, probably stopped between plays and said to themselves, yeah, old Robbie Hughes, he's dying. Even the cheerleaders.

So in the woods we cut a couple of beech trees and measured them out and I chained them and dragged them with the Farmall out to the dock at the edge of the woods, all the time feeling that baggie in my pocket. When I went back he was standing there and I knew by the set of his body that he wanted to try it now. He jerked his head which meant let's go to the ash grove, and so we went, crunching through the leaves and dry twigs. When we got there we sat on our log, the one we always sat on, and I took the bag out.

"D'jou get it?"

"Buddy Case."

"But he's—" and he shook his head. He meant that Buddy Case came from a good family who would be shocked at this.

I got out the paper and started to roll one while he watched. When I finished I got out a pack of matches.

"Make yourself one," he said. "I ain't doin' this alone."

"No, we share this one."

"Ain't but a pinch in there."

"It's enough."

I showed him how. He took a deep puff and held it in his lungs, as I did. Then again. After a minute he said, "I don't feel nothin'. ...'zat like shredded spinach or what?"

"Wait," I said.

While we sat I remembered how when I was little we drove out on the dirt roads near our three hundred acres of woodland and he went up a hill and stopped the car. "See," he said, "how you can tell they're ash trees?" and he pointed, and sure enough off in the distance you could see the top of the grove, lighter than the maple and hemlock trees trees around it, and higher, and while he studied it I knew he was worried that someone would see it too and go up there with a tractor and chainsaw and take a couple because of the board foot value of ash. Nobody ever did, but he was always worried.

I looked over at him and he was staring at the trees, his mouth part open like he was either trying to remember something or as if something had just occurred to him.

"I see my hearing," he said.

"What?"

"I hear a bird and at the same time I see a coil that flashes at it. That is my hearing. I mean like a bright corkscrew? You can see through it though."

"Okay," I said. My voice was a boy's voice that came

from the trees, kind of high-pitched and distant. "I think I see it too, like shimmering?" I couldn't lower my voice.

"That's it," he said. "A coil."

His voice came from there too. Then I looked at his hands, sawdust in the hair on the backs, palms and joints polished and shining from gripping tools all his life. I stared at them.

After a while, I don't know how long, he said, "I thought maybe it would be like a thing they could replace, you know, the size of a lighter."

"Oh."

"I mean what with all you see on the TV."

There was another silence while I tried to figure out what he had said. It was a long silence that felt more or less normal. Later on I figured he was talking about a pancreas.

It was bright, sort of shimmering, and I couldn't figure out what was happening with the columns of light coming through the ash trees. "I can see the light shooting down," I said, and he flinched sort of, because he had been traveling around in that silence. "Like streams of water. Can you do that?"

And he said, "Does time run through you or do you run through time? I mean, the sun ain't moved at all and we been here for what? A couple hours? I mean it slowed down a little, or not a little, a lot."

The light was like a liquid and I could easily see it. It raced right into the ground and did nothing to it.

"I know," he said. "It stopped. But then there'd be no night, you know?"

"Yes."

"How far away is the house?"

"The light isn't particles really," I said. "Not beams either. It's a solid. I mean it—"

"Right now I lost weight," he said. "Can you do that?"

"I think you can."

"What is that lady's name? The weight lady?"

"I think it's Jenny?"

"That's her," he said. "Anyway—" and he gestured at the trees, his hand leaving a trail of hands behind it, maybe twenty of them all lined up overlapping each other in transparent superimposition representing the sweep of that gesture, all of them hovering there for a second before they faded.

"That was amazing," I said.

"Ma's gonna be mad," he said. "We missed dinner." He held his fist out to me. "...'at make sense to you? Letters instead of numbers and the arrows all bent like that?"

It was his watch. I squinted at it, trying to focus. It was 2:45. "It's only 2:45," I said.

"I think we made a mistake," he said. Then he shook his head. "How many of those round files I use to sharpen the chain have I lost around here?"

"A bunch," I said. "I mean, hell, fifteen, eighteen?"

"Gotta be time to eat," he said. "Gotta."

A little later we went back, me driving the Farmall and him standing on the drawbar. In the kitchen he splashed water on his face and went into the living room to look at the paper. My mother watched him, then looked at me with a what have you been doing? look and I held my shoulders up in a sustained shrug and said, "Hey, like—" and then gestured around me, and she squinted and then clicked her tongue. Then I went up to the barn. Her look meant have you been drinking or doing some other such thing you shouldn't and my hey meant don't worry, leave it alone, because he hasn't got that much time and it wasn't any harm, and her final click of the tongue said "Okay, but don't do something stupid."

At the place at the back of the barn I stood and looked at the leaves, thinking about what we had just done, and then heard the creak of his step at the other end. "...'sup?" I said.

"How much more of that you got?" he asked.

We sat in the ash grove like that every two or three days, as if he sort of waited until the time was right. By the fifth time the log had two hard, shiny spots where we sat, and he started worrying about me. "This can't be good for you," he said.

"Nah, no harm."

"Promise me you won't do it after."

You're gone, I thought. "I won't."

"I mean unless—"

"Okay." Unless I got into the kind of fix he was in.

And after we sat, there would be the silence, the shafts of light, the sudden, remarkable changes where either I or he would realize that we tasted what we heard, or could feel what we saw on our eyes so that he claimed that seeing something really bad might do physical damage, or whatever.

And he would say only short things at first—hey, I am welded to this log. Why? or Eyesight is wrong, because stuff far away isn't really small, so why don't we see it in its real size? Isn't that a flaw? Or, I ain't buyin' any more boots. When you do, don't skimp—and gradually, across long silences, he would say more. This would just start, making me stare at his profile as he spoke, apparently to the trees.

"All time really is there and what happens is we just get to move through a little part of it. That's what's wrong."

"But—"

"So right now Lincoln is chopping some wood and this log is standing straight up but we just don't get to move through that part of it. We move only through our part of it. You know how it is when you dream, you see things that you could never see when you're awake, but what happens now is me being awake and dreaming at the same time, but anyway, my problem is bein' locked into my track that runs from here to over there, and—"

"But—"

"—everything is always there, even way back however far you want to go, so this ain't really that bad when you think that everybody has his own track that runs from here to over there and everything was always here, even things that ain't happened yet, at least for me, an' you an' me, well, we're on our little tracks that run from here to over there an' we don't ever get to see any of the rest but does that really matter? I see a ball with all these threads starting at the middle going outward but the ball never ends and each thread—I mean if I was to live to be a hundred, it would be still my own thread that runs from here to over there."

"I see." I looked at him, and his face was sort of eager and bright, like he was still trying to level up what he had just said. "That's more'n I ever heard you say in one lump."

He looked at me. "How'd you do that?"

"What?"

"See me think? I din' think you could do that."

"That's okay."

Toward the end my mother told a neighbor that my dad had made peace with God. I was glad she saw it that way, but I would have said he had made his peace with the world and himself. When we couldn't go to the ash grove any more I'd find the right opportunity, like when my brothers were off at their friends' houses and she went shopping, and roll one sitting right there by his bed downstairs, one of those hospital beds they gave us, and although I am sure my mother could smell what I couldn't get out the window by flapping a towel, she never said any- thing. She made clicking sounds, squinted at me.

I saw things the way he did. When he died I thought of it as his thread running out, and for a couple of weeks, mid-November it was, there were a lot of people in our house, and I would go out to the barn and stand at that space at the back just to kind of level up my sense of time and kind of feel it. When that visiting activity was over I went on with the work as usual, and ended up one day in the ash grove, the zip lock bag in my jeans. I brushed the grit off the log, sat down, and rolled a thin joint, but couldn't light it because of the silence. I dug my heel in the mulch and buried the joint and the bag there and got up to leave, looking around first for any evidence of people—tracks, shotgun shells, whatever, but found none. But I was not convinced about the trees. Before leaving I looked around at them, the gray pillars supporting the now leafless frame for the canopy that would be back the next year, and realized it was my job now to keep a keen eye on them, to listen during the day for the telltale sounds of engines or chainsaws, to make sure all the posted signs were still there on the fence lines.

# Perfect Shot

Until my younger sister Stephanie was thirteen, my father was able to live his life according to the customary pattern of his pioneer ancestors. These were hard and angular people whose lives were given over to heavy rural labor, and, as far as the men were concerned, to their strongest passion: hunting. Their names had always been touchstones among the older hunting enthusiasts of the midsized backcountry town nearest us. At those feedstore gatherings on Saturday mornings their names would be uttered in a tone of almost mythic veneration, and my father was always regarded with a similar respect. He looked the part of the pioneer hunter too—he was a burly man with black hair on his arms and the backs of his hands, which was always ingrained with bits of feed dust and hay chaff. He had so heavy a beard that even after he shaved, his chin and cheeks would have the feeling and nearly the look of emery paper.

I saw myself a part of the cyclical movement of genera-
tions, ready to fit into my family's personal mythology.  I
could see it all sweeping backward in time—my grandfather, who lived in a little house a half a mile down the dirt
road from us, would come over on Saturdays and eventually draw Stephanie to the glass cabinet in the living room.
Inside were set up the little ornate black boxes which held
the gilt-framed daguerreotypes of our ancestors, peering
out at us from their lofty distance.  My grandfather would
lean over us as we sat on our knees in the thick aroma of
chewing tobacco, and name each one, pointing with his
hairy, gnarled hand—"and here's old uncle Reuben who
got the ten pointer whose rack you hang your coats on."
We would stare into the bony and stern faces, into the
pale discs of the eyes as flat as tin, and shift from side to
side so that the bleached, spectral forms would flash back
at us as they caught the dim light of the room.

But we were years past the middle of the century.  I
remember seeing the evidence of progress from the peculiar perspective of a brushy hill about a mile from our
house.  When I was eleven my father began letting me
follow him on his routine pheasant hunts, and one spring
afternoon he stopped me and pointed out a sickle-shaped
curve of highway peeking through the dense woodland,
and protected inside it, a shopping center which had just
opened, the tiny red and green and yellow lights blinking
at us.  Beyond those lights were squared-off lots with tract
houses lined up in the deadly precision of bales of hay in
a field.  It all seemed to me some kind of offensive line in
the garish, creeping attack of civilization at our flanks.

But for each of us the shopping center gradually developed a magnetic power, so that my mother would be
difficult to budge from the supermarket, Sephanie from
the pet shop, and, because I liked to draw and paint, I

could usually be found in the stationery store. My father would always wind up milling in the hardware store, musing over paints, peculiar new tools you would never see in the old town store, bright cans of spray insecticides. The shopping center seemed a distant enough threat, but the change it represented emerged in my sister, who, just after her thirteenth birthday, suddenly declared war on my father and on tradition itself.

Before this she had lived in her own world and accepted the hard facts of life, best represented by the once a month or two occasion of my father's going out for deer, with blissful disregard for the law. The result had always been the same: in the barn at dusk, in that fading copper light coming in through the doorway in a thick, dusty shaft, the deer would hang dripping blood, so that a cloud of black flies buzzed over the deep red wad of hay placed on the floor to soak it up. There would be that rich, metallic smell of butchered meat and viscera, the slap of the knife on the strop, and over in the corner, my grandfather getting ready with his scraping tools and soaking tubs to cure the hide.

Because of the idealistic standards of school library books Stephanie's vision of nature was that of most children—it was a humane, utopian world where little girls fed peanuts to fawns beside clear streams while sparrows fluttered above. To her, my father must have seemed as evil as the forest fire in Bambi, a tobacco-smelling monster with pheasants dangling obscenely from his belt, but she never complained. During the butchering she would sit and look into the decapitated buck's eyes, black pools containing a kind of liquid infinity, like deep space. She would pat its head and whisper to it as if it were still alive, while just behind her, my father would bring the cleaver down with a loud thwack making her flinch with vicarious pain and whisper at a quicker pace into the buck's ear.

To add to the mood of this picture, it is worth mentioning that she was a skinny and frail child, given to a multitude of sicknesses which kept my parents on edge for years. I recall my mother always looking for swelling glands under her jaw, and my father frequently interrupting her entrance into the kitchen by holding in front of her a glass of dark red juice from the roasting pan, which she would dutifully drink, her eyes closed and the bridge of her nose wrinkled in disgust and calm martyrdom.

The first suspicious manifestations of her emerging identity came when she was around twelve. At school, at one of the open houses, she had set up an elaborate and frighteningly gruesome photographic display of examples of man's cruelty—mutilated harp seals and whales, animal paws crushed in traps, the slaughter of magnificent African beasts, cars with bucks draped over fenders. It seemed to me a direct suggestion that my father and men like him added up to the collective epitome of man's barbarism. But the expression on his face was one of studied curiosity along with a look of some embarrassment at being around all the well-dressed town people. He didn't seem to get the message. He seemed more skeptical about my display—I had achieved a reputation as an artist, and when he looked at my paintings and drawings, of idyllic nature scenes and bottles and flowers, he suddenly twisted his face up in suspicious wonder. I flushed with shame, for the first time recognizing in myself behavior inconsistent with his vision of a healthy boyhood. He moved the red leather cap on his head and then scratched his chin, thinking. I stood there listening to the abrasive rasping of his nails, studied the back of his hand, still with bits of hay chaff caught in the hair. "They're just pictures," I said.

"They ain't bad," he said, and returned to my sister's project.

At home Stephanie began to collect animals, birds injured by cats, baby rabbits orphaned by the clattering sickle bar of the hay cutter, and once even a baby raccoon (my father got the parents). Twice it got into the old International truck and put the lights on. His eyes narrow with barely controlled rage as he uncoiled the jump cables, my father ordered her to keep it in the cage or lose it. A week later the raccoon got under the hood of the car and pulled all the plug wires off, and while it tried to clean the grease off its paws at the cedar water bucket on the porch, working with almost hysterical attention, my father leaned over the open hood cursing through his teeth trying to figure out which wires went to which plugs. Stephanie had to get rid of the raccoon, and it ended up as a pet at our central school. My father had had enough—he claimed that the coon was ruining the dogs, so that he would glare in exasperation at them as they dozed away the afternoon, the raccoon wandering around right in plain sight of their disinterested stares.

I think I existed between the two attitudes, that it was nice as far as I was concerned that the world of animals had a peaceful balance and I would like to have fed peanuts to a fawn, but this sentiment was easily overcome by my identification with my father and my dreams of continuing the family's tradition. The reality came the September I turned fourteen, when my father presented me with a beautiful, long-stocked Enfield .303. As I held it in my hands, examining the stock which was marred I imagined in honorable warfare, he lectured me as to its qualities. "That heft there makes it accurate. Can hit a chuck at two hundred yards with that." I would have preferred a Winchester like his, but it didn't matter, because with the same happy disregard for the law our family had lived by, I was going out to do as my father did.

The only problem was Stephanie. The closer I got to my first hunt the less she would speak to me. Her room was gradually becoming a dizzying cubicle of posters of dewy-eyed animals, and with a surly haughtiness, aggravated by her usual chest cold, she would throw me out whenever I wandered in.

A few days before my first trip we were eating supper, and my father and I speculated on where we should go. With the hunt approaching, I brought up the subject whenever I could, to the point that Stephanie would gaze at the ceiling in an impudent gesture of appeal to some higher authority. The law was something we wouldn't normally mention except that that night my sister looked up from a forkful of mashed potatoes, her face dead serious with speculative indignation, and said, "The laws are made for a reason, you know." Then she waved the potatoes out toward my father. "Killing warm-blooded animals is barbaric."

I came out with a manly guffaw. My father screwed his eyebrows together and smiled, thinking. "Barbaric?" he said. "What's barbaric about puttin' meat on the table?" Then he chewed with his eyes closed, enjoying the taste. He swallowed, nodded thoughtfully. "Those laws is made so we have to put up with Boston dentists and stockbrokers only once a year, that's what they're made for."

I laughed again, my cheeks stuffed with half-chewed venison.

"This is good with onions, missus," my father said.

And my mother said, "This is onions from Texas of all places. I got them at the supermarket."

"Mm," my father said, "dentists and psychiatrists all decked out in red, sneakin' up the road." He was remembering last year, in deer season. We had seen a man stalking up our road carrying a rifle and wearing clothes so new that we wouldn't have been surprised to see the tags flapping in the breeze. We had stood there at the window going purple with quiet laughter.

"That isn't the point," my sister said. "Deer, pheasants, raccoons—they don't do nobody any harm, 'n you go blow their brains out. The human race is a disease the planet has."

"Godalmighty, what you been readin'?" he said.

"I just see a bunch of stupid men with their shiny guns and it makes me sick." I had a little flash of fear and excitement. This was an insult more severe than anyone would ever dare to use with my father. But because he was the unquestioned patriarch of the family, he allowed it and went on chewing, dignified and oblivious.

"What if you're caught?"

"Fine," he said. "Don't know how much."

Then my sister rose and left the table. Gradually my father seemed to wake up, staring down the dark hallway, chewing in thoughtful slow motion. Caught? Fine? What the hell was she talking about? "What's she mean?" he asked.

"Let her alone," my mother said. "You know how she is. Besides, technically she's right."

I was full up in a stance of masculine indignation. My father stared at my mother, about to say something, but instead he shrugged and said, "Hey buck, pass me the peas, will you?"

I spoke to Stephanie later, in the living room, in a whisper my parents couldn't hear. "You better not."

"Better not what?" she said in a condescending whine.

"You'll get it good if you do."

"You know what you oughtta be able to do?" she said. "Look into their eyes before you kill them. That's all, just look into their eyes. You draw pictures. You're the one who's supposed to see."

"That's got nothin' to do with it."

"You'd probably gut shoot him."

"No way. I'm a good shot."

"Big deal," she said, and turned back to her magazine.

In the morning we left just after dawn, me cradling my .303 in the crook of my arm, my father with his 30-30 over his shoulder. There was one strange moment just after breakfast. There I was with my rifle, and on the couch were my sister, and my mother whispering instructions, initiating her into the secret mysteries of knitting, and when I saw them, their heads together, the needles waving like a beetle's feelers over the bright yarn, I felt that all was right with the world. But as we walked off toward the hedgerow Stephanie came out of the house wearing her red jacket. "I'd like to come too," she said.

"No, three's too many," my father said. "You stay."

"It's a free country," she said.

"Weather don't look good," he said in a tone tinged with sympathy.

"I am not sick!" she nearly shouted.

"No, you stay home," he said, his voice starting to sound a little exasperated. "Now this is a man's business."

Her face went red with anger and she glared at us with a kind of confident hostility I had not seen before. She suddenly looked peculiarly capable. I think my father must have noticed it too, because he sighed in apparent confusion and said, "Listen, if you want to go, fine. But not today, okay?" This bit of diplomacy didn't work. She snorted and went back into the house.

We walked. Early in that trip I recall one moment when I walked through some dried timothy toward a hillock, and stopped. Down around my feet were about nine or ten little partridge chicks, cheeping and darting through the grass, frightened by the towering figure above them but not knowing where to go. I thought of them as nervous little messengers of my sister's convictions. It was a strange moment, one I would later think of as an ironic pastoral in the manner of Wyeth, a canvas centered with a foreshortened body, gun barrel and feet, with the little chicks in the grass below. It made my breath halt, so that I stood stock still and watched them until my father, some distance away, waved me on with impatient jerks of his arm. So I tiptoed from their midst, careful not to step on any of them.

My father was the type who hunted in silence, keeping his attention to business, so we didn't talk until we stopped to eat the sandwiches my mother made the night before. He drew them out of his coat pocket, handed me mine, and said, "Next is that big draw over there below where you can see the shopping center. We'll go there first."

"Would it have been too much trouble to let Steph come?"

He paused with exaggerated tolerance. "Don't you pay that no mind," he said. "This is not a woman's business."

We went on, up over the wooded hills and through dead pastures and brush to that point where we could see the shopping center inside that arc of highway. He looked at it once, sighed, shook his head and waved me on. Our movement would take us to within a quarter of a mile of the highway, and there I felt the sensation of being in an alien place.

So the time came for me to see the buck, about a hundred yards away, head down, partly blocked by brush. "Six, maybe eight point," my father said. "He's yours, git on."

"Straight?"

He sighed. Where was all the education he pumped into me? "Wind," he whispered. "C'mon."

"It's toward us, from him. Straight." He nodded, and I crept forward. He had told me that a deer trusts his smell more than his eyes sometimes, so he'll see you and not worry too much, but if he smells you, he's gone.

When the time came for me to raise the rifle I could feel my father's eyes on my back—forty yards, and I set, aimed and fired, and then stood in awe as the buck rose and bolted powerfully, the light amber flank muscles rippling, and in two magnificent jumps he was gone over a barbed wire fence, flashing his white tail back at us. When I turned, my father was looking at me with a strange expression on his face. Forty yards? He sighed again, his eyebrows up in the middle of his forehead, and said, "Well, we all miss, one time 'r another."

I followed him back in gloomy shame. As was appropriate, we saw no more deer that day. Instead our progress back toward home was interrupted by a good-natured man in khaki.

"What are you hunting for today?"

"Woodchucks," my father said, his voice dry with objectivity.

"Strange place for it," the man said. "Pasture's back there."

"Why do you ask?" my father said.

He was a game warden. My father stood and answered his questions mechanically, and we went on toward home. I could see that in a short time he was fuming, walking so fast that I had to trot to keep up. And I was thinking, she did it, she went and did it. Called the goddamned game warden. I suppose I let myself become livid with anger because it was a reasonable replacement for the shame I felt earlier. I had no idea what my father planned. A spanking? She was probably too old for that. The one time I did speak to him on the way I said, "Lucky I missed, huh?" But he had no comment about that.

As we approached the house I started to get a little shaky about the prospect of a confrontation, and the purposeful stride of my father ahead of me seemed aimed straight at her. She had been asking for it anyway. But underneath I felt sorry for her too—the frail one had gone too far this time, and although punishment seemed just, I hoped it would not be too harsh.

Then came the straw that broke the camel's back. A careful man with guns, my father put up the Winchester in the case in the woodshed and as a matter of habit broke his twenty gauge shotgun to check to see if it was empty— there, where the barrel drooped and separated from the base and firing pin, was a wad of bubble gum spreading out, pink and sweet smelling. He gazed at it, stunned. Inside the house the vacuum cleaner started up, in the living room probably. My father stood looking at the gum spreading in threads and webs in the chamber of his twenty gauge, blinking, the blood boiling up into his face. My knees were weak. She's crazy, I thought, absolutely crazy.

He placed the shotgun on the workbench, turned with a wooden-backed rigidity, and went toward the door. I put my rifle down and went behind him. "Listen, I'll clean it," I said. "I'll clean it. She was mad is all. She just got mad."

He walked on through the kitchen, down the hall toward the scream of the vacuum. She was busily grinding away at the rug with the cleaner, while behind her my mother dusted the cabinet which held the old photographs. Speechless with rage, my father entered the room and advanced toward Stephanie, pointing his finger like a gun, and she saw him and turned the cleaner off, so that suddenly we all stood there in that huge, dusty silence. She rose from her stoop, and folded her arms. Then she looked at us, and there was something about her that made my father seem to momentarily forget what it was that he had planned to say. She had on dungarees and a halter and a bandanna around her hair, and her forehead was beaded with a fine sheen of sweat. It could have been the regal upsweep above her forehead, or the haughty, confident set of her body, or the way her arms were folded, but my father's arm slowly drooped to his side. She was suddenly formidable. He looked at her as if she were a stranger, as I did. She even had breasts. Of course I had noticed this before, but not in the same way that I did now. My father turned slowly toward me, his face held in a look of vague confusion, and walked out of the room. Nothing about this confrontation was ever mentioned. We never did find out if she had called the game warden, or if he happened to be there by accident. I suspect my father preferred not to know. He began gradually to complain about the usual aches and pains of advancing age, and our evening meals were cordial and gradually became normal. The next time my father's blood got the desire to go for illegal deer, he told me that it was too bad, the world was changing, that the shopping center was just the beginning, and from now on it'd be wiser to wait for hunting season.

As for me, the one secret about all this that I have kept is that when I fired the rifle that day my aim was perfect—in the wide parabola of air between the lowered neck and the front legs, either out of respect for Stephanie's convictions, or the law, or the impressive visual beauty of the buck, I am not sure. It was a decision made in a split second and on half-conscious impulse. I would get my bucks later, during deer season and with a minimum of complaint from my sister, and we would continue to eat venison, but it is sure that we were finished living the privileged existence of our ancestors.

# Some Things
# That Can't Be Helped

While the kids, his younger brother and sister among them, filed up the front steps and into the school, he waited near the bus with his breath held against the white exhaust curling up around him. He watched the windows of the principal's office, and when the bus pulled out to turn at the end of the school driveway, he walked behind it and turned toward the town, to go and see the dentist about his sister's tooth. If the dentist would accept a note from his mother, would he fix the cavity in her tooth and accept payment from him? His mother, he would explain, was unable to come to town because she was sick, and the cavity in Becky's tooth was bad enough that something needed to be done before she lost the tooth.

Walking, he ran his tongue over his own teeth, thinking that he could use a dentist, too. But he had to cover Becky first, and Ron's teeth seemed okay, although he didn't brush them enough. He picked up his pace, bothered a little by the condition of his clothes, somewhat darkened with grime on the thighs of his jeans and smelling of pinesap and gasoline.

The dentist's office was on the ground floor of a large house in the nicest part of the town. He stopped at the door: Samuel Danks, DDS. He took a deep breath and let it out, and then opened the door. Behind a desk sat Mrs. Hoag, who was the mother of one of the girls in his class. She looked up. "Can I help you?" She apparently didn't recognize him.

"I want to find out about getting my sister's tooth filled. Front one."

The woman looked down at a piece of paper, and then up again. "How old is she?"

"Thirteen."

"Your parents should be here."

"My mother's sick, and says that if you need it, she'll write a note. She'll pay cash if it's not too—well, expensive." The woman thought about this, and then got up and went into another office.

She came back out. "Dr. Danks says that will be all right, but first he has to examine the tooth, and your mother has to sign a form."

"Can I take the form to her and have her sign it? It's hard for her to get here."

"Yes, assuming that it's a routine procedure."

"And do you have, like, an estimate of the cost of a routine procedure?"


The walk back home was nine miles if he didn't get a ride. This time, though, he got one from an old man who lived in the tiny village five miles from their place, which was on a wooded hilltop far from any other houses. The old man had written a book, he recalled, about how the area was in the early part of the century, and he got ready to ask him three times about his book, but the radio— WDOS Oneonta—was on, and the old man seemed interested in hearing news about the Middle East and terrorists. "Here you go, son," he said, pulling over at the crossroads of the village. He thanked the man and got out. With five miles to go, he wondered if he should walk on over to the village's 7-Eleven to check out their sale things, but decided against it because he had to get back home.

The hike up the long, winding dirt road was so familiar, and he had done it so many times, that he felt as if he slept as he went. There was Munson's, caved into its own foundation, and then Richardson's, still standing but boarded up in the windows, and then two places that had been no more than piles of gray wood in foundations since he could remember, then a fairly good-looking place owned by a family that had moved in a couple years earlier and whom they didn't know. Then it was the last, flat mile on the top of the hill to his house. By the time he got there he was tired, felt almost old in his legs. He pushed the kitchen door open and went inside. There, looking around at the faded walls and the rusted electric stove, he decided he'd make some instant coffee.

But he had to call his mother first. The number was in his wallet, with the 561 area code for Florida. He lifted the receiver off the wall and poked out the numbers, and waited, hoping it would be his mother and not Rocky Case. It was his mother.

"It's me," he said.

"Oh, how are you all doing?" He heard a TV in the background.

"Not so good. Look," and he tried to think of a way

to put it, because her voice was thick. She was drunk. "Becky's gotta get a tooth filled. Front one."

"Oh the poor baby," his mother said.

"Could you send up some money? I mean we're really sorta scratchin' up here, and I don't know—"

"Oh, I'll send some," she said. "Soon as we can."

"I know. You said that last time. We didn't see any, and it isn't enough to cut logs and pulpwood. There's the mortgage and the electricity and all that. Taxes I don't know what to do about. We got some kind of a tax bill. What do I do with that?"

"Well, you send money I guess."

"Are you coming back sometime soon? I mean it's been, like, more than a month."

There was a silence with faint TV voices in the background, then a sigh. "Danny honey," she said. "We can't help ourselves. God knows we would if we could. But we can't. For me it's a struggle to get up in the morning, and Rocky, well, he's trying, but nothing we do works. He's trying working at a gas station. Working right now. But me, I'm unable to even get dressed." She coughed, and then laughed with a throaty cynicism. "The world's falling apart and we're going with it, I'll tell you."

"Okay."

"God knows I'd help if I could, and I'll tell you what— I'll find a way to send some money right away. Promise."

"Okay."

"You're supposed to be in school aren't you? Today's Monday, right?"

"Yeah, but I can't. I gotta cut wood."

"You be careful with that, will you?"

"I will."

"Gives me nightmares," she said. "I don't want that to happen to you."

"It won't. I'll be careful."

"I wish there was some way I could help. But I'll be honest. I thought Florida would be a new start, and it isn't. I feel guilty about leaving you guys up there, but I had no choice. I don't know what to do about taxes or mortgages or teeth or anything else, you see? We don't have air conditioning down here, and without air conditioning, you can't even think. Rocky says the only time he feels good is when he's in the office at the station. The rest of the time he feels like he's sick. I feel like I'm sick all the time. I don't know what to do about that. But I'll send the money, promise. I promise."

"Okay."

"I wouldn't have left if there was any other way. But there wasn't any other way. There's nothing I can do."

"Okay. You heard from Roz?"

"A while ago. She says Vegas isn't what it's cracked up to be either. But she's working, and her boyfriend is too."

"Well, that's good. Is it the same boyfriend?"

"No, different. Better, she says."

"Okay."

"Well, you take care now."

"Yeah, you too."

So he made coffee and crossed that possibility off the list. Sitting at the table and sipping at the coffee, he calculated the time. Ten-thirty. He had four cords of pulp piled up on the dock by the road, and if Marty Wallace came up with his stake truck at five o'clock and saw only four cords, he would be more than irritated. There wasn't enough money in pulpwood. The money was in hard maple and ash. That thought sent a little surge of fear through him, which he knew was unwarranted. He got up and went to the cupboard over the stove and took out a handful of trailmix bars, stuffed them into his jeans pockets and went outside to the tractor. In the heavy wagon hitched to it were the chainsaw, gas, oil, the round file he used to sharpen the chain, and the cant hook. Six cords would be over two hundred dollars. The tooth might cost a hundred. The tax bill was thirty-five and change.

They had a hundred seventy-five acres of woodland, which surrounded what had once been a small dairy farm, like the other places on the road. The dairy business had failed for all of them in the fifties and sixties, and those people who didn't torch their barns for the insurance money ended up cutting pulpwood and logs, or worked for the county road. The smart people, he supposed, had all left.

Their family had been more or less normal, the four kids going to the central school in town, nine miles away. When he was fourteen he had dreamed of playing football, like a lot of the other boys. He had actually liked school, but that all changed when his sister Roz became a whore and his father died. The correspondence of those two events rested in his memory as almost simultaneous, although he realized the separation was three months or even more. Roz had gone with three boys in a van and had taken them all on, and the school was of course in a buzz about that the Monday after. The boys had passed the story around so much that by the time he had arrived at school on Monday, everybody knew. Some kid had spray painted the side of the bus garage with the somewhat mysterious message, *RL the legend–16*. Before lunch he had found out what it meant. She had done it sixteen times, and there were whispers and animated talk in small groups in the halls, talk that would pause as he walked past, the eyes of the boys on him with a wary, sort of gleeful patience, waiting for him to be out of earshot so they could go on with the story. At the end of the day, waiting outside for the bus, he saw two of the tougher boys looking at him, having paused before getting into their old Jeep. They were on the football team, and he didn't want to mess with them. He shrugged amiably, but that didn't satisfy them. One took a couple of steps toward him and said, "Hey Danny-boy? You pissed? Your regular jumped the fence, dude."

The result was a fight, witnessed it seemed by everyone he worried about in terms of his self respect, and despite his managing to get one good shot on the boy's shoulder, he ended up on the ground fighting the urge to cry. When the boy told him to get up, he shook his head, and the boy yelled out, "Fuckin' chicken we got here. Fuckin' bum of a chicken." The principal then came out to break it up, and somehow, in the discussion, it was Danny who ended up the instigator. After all, they didn't want their football players suspended from school, so he decided, sitting there in the school driveway, to suspend himself. It didn't matter. At home later, the same day of the fight, he looked in the mirror at the dried blood around the rim of his nostril and let all that shit go. He let go of the worry about his appearance, his clothes, his friendships with various kids at school, his deferential behavior in the presence of one girl or another that he thought he liked. None of that stuff could be his anymore.

That was when he began to worry about his younger sister and brother. He wanted to make sure that their clothes looked right. He wanted to make sure that they had enough money for lunch. His mother didn't seem to care. She spent her time watching TV and drinking, all day, while his father, revving himself up in the morning with a few belts, eventually made his way to the woods to cut pulpwood or logs. Whatever his problems in school, they didn't care, and didn't care what the younger kids looked like either. Roz was Roz—she acted as if either nothing had happened, or if it did, it didn't matter.

One day in the woods in late spring, he was trimming a maple with the double-bitted axe when he heard the chainsaw fifty yards away suddenly lug down and sputter, and the sound was followed by a loud crack. The chainsaw sputtered off, and he had decided to continue trimming until the silence began to bother him, so he dropped the axe and went to where his father was working. Making his way into the clearing, he saw him standing against one ash tree with another tree right there in front of him, attached to the stump by a thick split section that swept up the tree like a large, bent plank, the pale wood gleaming. Ash was straight grained, and that was always a problem with it. It looked as if his father were hiding behind the one he had cut, his cheek against the rough, pale bark, and when Danny went closer to see what was going on, the wind in the treetop pivoted the twenty-inch trunk a little, rolling into his father's chest. He was dead, his mouth filled with something mushy and deep-red that had been forced up by the trunk crushing his torso against the other tree, and Danny stood there looking, his breath held, as whatever was in his mouth surged outward and then back with the top of the tree swinging in the wind.

Within four months, with the funeral still what seemed right behind them, Roz moved away with her boyfriend and Rocky Case moved in. Rocky had lived in a small trailer by the little town and was well known as a loser, but also as a good, fun-loving guy. And within a month of moving in, he had taken over as if he were the father, responsible for disciplining the kids. The guy tried being sort of familiar with everyone, as if he'd known them all their lives. His mother tried to mediate everything, from his threatening Danny with a belt for some infraction that meant nothing, to regulating what Becky wore to school. Once, when Danny was not at home, there had been some sort of a discipline thing involving her clothes, and Rocky ended up hitting her. Danny got home just as they were finishing talking about it in the kitchen, his mother crying and Rocky Case standing there with his arms folded and looking at Danny as if he were some stranger who happened to walk into the kitchen. Danny shrugged and left, so that they could continue their stupid discussion. And he didn't like the way Rocky Case looked at Becky, either. He could see the man watch her walking through the living room or, through the bathroom doorway, brushing her hair. Why they took off for Florida he didn't know, unless it was something to do with better access to alcohol.

Any tree less than a foot thick at the base. Beech, maple, birch, not hemlock. He cut six of them down and marked them off with the measuring stick using the axe, and in three hours had enough pulp to make two more full cords. Calculating the time, he figured he had to stop there and endure Marty's skeptical looks when he came up with the truck.

"Here you go, kid," Marty said, handing him the bills.

"Thanks."

"So how's your ma?"

Danny shrugged and looked away at the dirt road. "Lookin' for a job up Utica," he said. "Tough these days, what with nine-eleven and all."

Marty snorted. "Nine-eleven don't mean nothin' here."

"No, I mean like your trickle-down effect. Means jobs get scarce. Leastways the kind she looks for."

Marty nodded. "Look, I can't come up unless there's more, okay? I mean, logs, maybe, if they're eighteens or better. Or if they're ash?"

"Got ash."

"Okay, then you're still in business. Next week?"

"Yeah. No, I can have some by say Thursday."

"You gotta be sure. The gas just to come up here is a lot."

"I'm sure. I can have a three-hundred dollar load by then."

He watched as Marty pulled away, and watched as the stake truck passed under the branches of the trees that made the road a sun-dappled tunnel. Just as the truck went out of view, leaving billows of dust, the school bus emerged from the dust coming his way. Rather than stand there, he went up the drive and into the house. No point in having Mrs. Bremner see him so that she could report it to the school the next day.

Becky and Ron walked up the dirt driveway, both leaning forward against the weight of their backpacks. Having been alone all day, he didn't mind that they were home. They made their way into the kitchen and dropped their packs on the floor. They went to the refrigerator.

"No soda," Danny said. "We ran out."

"There's Kool Aid," Becky said. "Yuk." Danny watched her as she scanned the stuff in the refrigerator. She was built like Roz, maybe a little too what they called voluptuous, and it didn't help that she wore the tight jeans slung low so that her belly-button showed. But a lot of the girls enjoyed showing it off, and he supposed Becky wasn't any different.

"Kool Aid's for dorks," she said.

"I'll be the dork," Ron said, and took the plastic container out.

"Sometime this week you can get your tooth done," Danny said. "I got a note in the mail from Ma. We gotta set up an appointment."

"Can't she just come down? Can I call her?"

"I know. Utica's only fifty miles away, but she's lookin' for a job. Can't call either. They got no phone."

"Then I ain't goin'."

"Yes you are. A cavity is—well, like low-class. You can't have a cavity. The kids at school don't."

"Shit," she said.

"You're not supposed to curse either."

"Shit," Ron said.

Danny laughed. "Okay."

"Let's check the TV," Becky said, heading for the living room. Ron followed her.

"You're supposed to do homework first," he called after them.

"Fuck homework," Becky called.

Later, while three TV dinners heated up in the oven, Danny helped Becky write a paper about the clash of religions in the Middle East, and what Christians should think about that. Then he sat at his desk, in his room, and worked on the note. He had fifteen tries piled up on the right, and worked on the sixteenth, trying to copy, exactly, the somewhat girly style of his mother's writing: the rounded letters, the exact up-and-down quality of the loops, the offset dots over all the i's. His model was an old note she had written for him, excusing him from school because his parents were sick. He remembered that—his mother and father had been in a particularly bad phase of getting too drunk every night, and his mother had wanted him around during the day to help his father cut wood, because she feared that he wasn't being careful with the chainsaw and the falling trees. That was a time when he had felt anxious about missing school, and anxious about the problems in the family remaining secret. It didn't matter now. Everything was out of the bag now, and his ruse of claiming that his mother was in Utica was no more than a strategy on his part to make more legitimate his use of forged notes, and his authority over the kids. If they had known she was in Florida, or if the school had known, then that authority would be eroded. He was seventeen, one year away from being safe from the State's meddling. Had the State known, they'd probably be shipped off to foster care somewhere. He didn't want that.

He would skip school again tomorrow. Call about the appointment for Becky's tooth and take the day to cut ash trees. The thought sent a surge of fear through him, because he would be working in that stretch of woods where his father had been killed. It occurred to him that the tree that had killed him was still standing there, its canopy of branches and dead leaves tangled in with other trees. The police and fire-rescue people who had come to collect the body had worked him out from between the two trunks, looking up and watching to make sure the tree wouldn't fall. That seemed kind of a blur now, watching the men do that, while other things about the death remained very clear. One image he could not shake was of his father's face, with that stuff crowding his mouth and surging out and receding as the tree, pushed by the wind, groaned against him.

Despite the wind since the accident, the tree still stood there. Now, thinking practically, he calculated the tree's value—it was forty or more feet of good log, even with the split slab. But there was no way to get it to fall. He went beyond that tree, checking spaces between trees to make sure that, once he found a good one, he'd be able to get the tractor to it.

He found an ash tree, maybe not quite twenty across at the trunk but high enough to qualify. They were beautiful trees, rising higher than the maples or beeches, their trunks decreasing in circumference only slightly. When he started the chainsaw and gauged the wind and the slight tilt, and the balance of leaves and branches in the top, he paused before taking the first big chip out, because the last time they had cut an ash tree his father ended up dead. But he had to ignore that, and went on with it, going to the back side and cutting in, the chainsaw vibrating his hands and the exhaust curling around his face. When the coarse sawdust had just begun to cover his left shoe, which was right at the trunk base, he saw the chip on the other side begin to close, heard the snapping sounds inside, and ran the blade of the saw in farther to prevent any splits before pulling away. He walked backwards fifteen feet, watching the tree topple, and then it swished down through the branches of other trees, taking them with it, and slammed onto the mulchy soil, its cut end bouncing up a good twenty feet before coming to rest. A large shaft of sunlight now illuminated the area. He would cut two maples he had seen, fairly big ones, and together that would make enough in board feet to make Marty's trip up the hill worth it. In the early afternoon, he was dragging the logs, one by one, out to the lower loading dock at the edge of the woods. His back hurt, his hands hurt, and the labor of rolling the logs up the incline with the cant hook so that they could drop into the huge wagon bed sapped him so much that, after he transferred them the six hundred yards up through the meadow to the dock by the road, he decided to park the wagon by the road dock and transfer the logs the next day. He called and got an appointment for Becky, but on Friday of the following week, and the estimate was eighty dollars, which he had.

He was ready to go out and work on the logs the next morning, having passed on getting on the bus, when his mother called. "Oh that's wonderful about her tooth. You did that all by yourself?"

"Yeah. It's Danks over to town."

"Well, like I was saying, we're coming up for just a little while. Rocky's got a car he wants to sell, and I want to see you guys and make sure everything's okay."

"Okay," he said. "Why doesn't he sell the car down there?"

"Oh no, you don't understand. We come up to see you guys. We need a car for that, but we need to sell it too. So he gets this idea, right? Why don't we drive up there and sell it in New York where we'll get more money for it? Take a little vacation and then take the bus back. We should be there by Thursday."

"Okay."

"I'm still looking for a job. I mean, sorta looking?"

"Yeah."

"I feel irresponsible, you know, but there are some things that can't be helped. I want to do right but that just seems a little out of reach right now? Rocky says not to worry about it. We'll surface. He says when you're down the way we are, you have to just ride with it until you're up." There was a silence. Then she said, "You don't sound convinced."

"No, it's not that. It's that I got to get logs up on the dock."

"Oh, I just thought you didn't believe me."

"I believe you."

"Just be sure and tell the kids that it's Utica. The car'll have a Florida license plate, but it's Utica, okay?"

"Sure."


The incline to the dock was around ten degrees, but the ash, particularly, was so heavy that it took him a half an hour to roll it up, pushing so hard on the handle of the cant hook that he thought he might break it. But he got them all in place within an hour and a half. After that he walked to the little village with some of the remaining money in his pocket to buy a money order for the taxes, a six-pack of soda and some chips. Then he walked home, the loops of the plastic bag digging into his fingers. By the time he had walked back up the hill and home, the bus was only a few minutes away.

He told them while they were looking in the refrigerator. The presence of the soda excited them a little, but when he mentioned their mother and Rocky coming home, Becky stopped and looked at the aluminum can. Then she went into the living room to watch TV. Ron snorted. "Well, it was fun. But it ain't gonna be when he starts up again. I mean he's fun and all, but—"

"You mean *isn't*," Danny said. "You just gotta do what you're told."

"Who's he think he is anyway? He acts like he owns this place."

"Does, in a way, I guess."

"They aren't married."

"I know, but for all practical purposes, they might as well be."

"Shit," Ron said.

"You can say that again."

The sitcoms were funny, but Becky didn't laugh. Danny watched her profile as they watched the television, and then he started to worry about what that meant. When the time came for homework, she asked him for help. "It's a revision of the last paper, the one on the Trade Towers? I got a C on it and she says I can do it over for a better grade."

"Okay," he said. "Lemme have it and we'll see."

"She didn't mark it up. She said I had to figure out what was wrong with it."

He sighed. "Okay, let's—" He looked around. Ron was going on watching TV. "What about you? You got homework?"

"Nope. Squat."

They sat at the kitchen table. The teacher had written 'content okay—grammar and structure horrible'. He laughed, and said, "We can fix this easy."

"It's more fun without him here," she whispered.

The expression of a kind of speculative awe on her face was not one of her normal expressions. He sat up straight and stared at the table. "What'd he do?"

"Ma doesn't want anyone to know."

"What'd he do?"

"Nothin', actually. It's what he said he has to do."

"What's 'at mean?"

She looked again at her paper, then up at him. "He's always sorta touchin' me when I go to bed and Ma and him come in to say goodnight and all that. Then one day he says we're goin' on a picnic, just him and me, because he wants to get to know the kids like individually he says. He's kinda drunk too. Ma starts to cry, and then he gets all mad. She's like, 'I know what you want to do,' an' he says, well—" She stopped there.

"He says?"

"He's all like so what? He says it's just the way it is, look at her. He says there's nothin' he can do about it. It's just the way it is. He says if we lived in some town in someplace like Colorado, where girls my age are given to 'elders' he called it, it would be an honor sorta."

"Colorado?"

"Well, someplace out there. Some town he mentioned."

"It's a crime you know."

"So what does Ma say? She says if I mention this at school she'll kill herself. She says she can't go through this again, what with Roz and all. She says to Rocky, you can't do that, and he says, how are you gonna stop me? How do I stop myself? It's the way it is. Morals and all that stuff are invented by people afraid to live, and then he says to me, you afraid to live? And Ma cries and says you can't. And he says there isn't any way it can be stopped. It's just how it is, and if we don't go on a picnic now, we'll go on one later. Doesn't make any difference. It's like the basic way things are."

"We gotta talk to somebody." He thought about that, about letting the cat out of the bag, and all he felt was a kind of anticipatory shame.

"No," she whispered. "We can't. Besides, they're only comin' for a few days you said, right?"

"You can't go on anything they say."

"I can lock my door." She thought a moment. "Actually, I talked to Ma and she said he only acts that way when he's drunk. He'd never say that stuff sober, she said. So she said I was to forget it."

He looked down at the paper. "I got an idea. What's her name? Martina, that friend of yours? Can you stay at her house?"

"Maybe," she said. "I don't know."

"There's gotta be an excuse. If she says you can, I can write a note."

"They're not gonna believe a note from you."

"No, I can fake it with mom's writing." He looked again at the paper. "I'll say you and Martina are doin' some project on—say, Middle Eastern religion."


The idea had seemed to him to make such obvious sense that he began getting anxious about Becky's putting it off, to the point that it appeared unlikely that she would go through with it. He continued cutting logs, assuming that Marty Wallace would see enough in the load he had cut to agree to come the following week. The electricity bill was past due, and he had to keep buying food. So he wrapped himself up in the familiar routine of the powerful vibration of the chainsaw in his hands, the feel of the axe handle as he trimmed, the smells of gas and oil and sap. And it was on the day that he began dragging logs from deep in the woods to the first dock at the edge, six hundred yards from the road and the house, that he saw the glint of a vehicle in the driveway.

He left everything in the woods and took the old Farmall tractor up the hill toward the house. Even from a distance, standing up before the wheel, he could tell that it was a Ford Explorer, new and white, and he wondered how it was that they'd been able to buy that.

They heard the tractor, apparently, because they were already out on the front porch when he was a hundred yards from the dirt road. His mother waved. Rocky stood there holding a cigarette, and nodded at him when he got to the road. He parked the tractor next to the road dock.

"You're lookin' good," his mother called.  "Kids at school?"

"Yeah," he called.

"How you doin'?" Rocky said.

"Fine."  His mother came down the driveway to him and hugged him.  "So how much did this cost?" he asked, pointing at the car.

"Great deal," she said.  "Nineteen.  It's two years old, but good condition."  He looked at her.  She had a tan, as did Rocky, and she looked just a little heavier than when they had left.  Rocky had on a bright blue print shirt with sailboats on it.

"Keyless entry," Rocky said.

"Really," Danny said.  "It's a cool lookin' car."

"So whatcha doin'?" Rocky asked.  "Cutting logs?"

"Yup.  Pays the bills."

"You're not in school," his mother said.

"Rather have electricity," he said.  "Which, by the way, I gotta pay for today."

"That load on the dock," Rocky said.  "How much that bring?  Is that an ash log?"

"Yeah.  Two-twenty.  I mean for the whole load."

"Not bad," he said, staring at the logs.  "That ain't bad at all.  And hell, what is it?  A hundred seventy acres?  You could go years in a spread that size."

"That's the idea," Danny said.  "I'm makin' sure to leave the middle sized ones, so they'll grow.  You know, timber management."

"Well, let's go inside," his mother said.

Things seemed reasonable enough.  As they talked in the kitchen, his mother and Rocky taking small drinks from a bottle of Jack Daniels sitting between them, Danny got the impression that maybe the Florida trip had done more good than bad for his mother.  She seemed positive about things. They talked about the possibility of Rocky's starting up some kind of a small business. Danny suggested that what they should do was truck stovewood down to New York City and sell it for ten times what they got from Marty Wallace, because Marty's small business was to send truckloads of the wood they cut, right here, and Danny pointed out the dusty window toward the woods. No, Rocky said, that wouldn't cut it. In fact, he'd been thinking that they should all go to Florida, sell this place and pull up stakes.

The idea made Danny get hot with disbelief. "It's all we got," he said.

"What?" Rocky said. "A patch of woods in the middle of nowhere? Come on, that's thinkin' small if I ever seen it."

"But what kind of a business would be better? This is good money."

"I haven't decided that one yet," Rocky said.

Danny's mother nodded, and said, "You give us time to figure this out. It'll work."

"I don't know," Danny said. "I'm not sure about that."

Rocky snorted. "You got no say in this anyway."

Danny got a sympathetic stare from his mother. Don't rock the boat.

So he wouldn't rock the boat. He told them that he still had to work on the next load, so he was going back down to the woods. There, working on trimming a maple tree and assessing where he would divide it for two logs, he stopped, and thought of Florida. He did not like the idea. He supposed the kids would. If it came to having to go, he would simply pass. But that idea wouldn't work either, because he'd be leaving Becky to go with them, and he didn't think that a guy who drank all the time was going to be able to help it if he got the notion to try something with her. He didn't think his mother would be able to help the situation either. He was back at trimming the tree when he heard the distant grinding of gears—Marty Wallace.

By the time he was out of the woods, standing again at the wheel of the tractor, he could see the truck up by the dock, could see two men working at rolling the logs onto the bed. It was Marty and Rocky. He looked at the shadow before him and figured it was only about two o'clock, which meant that Marty was early, by two hours at least.

When he got to the road Rocky was helping Marty with the last log. When it rolled down and slammed onto the truck bed, Marty went up with his cant hook and rolled it away from the edge while Rocky put the stakes back in their brackets. "Hey, thanks," Marty said. "We got two-fifteen here," and he took out his wallet, counted out the money, and gave it to Rocky.

"Deal," Rocky said.

"And the next load is what?" He looked at Danny.

"Couple days."

"I'll be here when you come by," Rocky said. "Hey, I got a question."

"Shoot," Marty said.

"Do people buy timberland around here?"

"Yeah. You go through Strout Realty."

"Strout."

"Not just pulpers either," Marty said. "There's people who buy it up and keep it, like for future logging and stuff. Can still cut the bad ones for firewood and truck it downstate. And there's tax breaks."

Rocky nodded, thinking. "Well, it's an idea," he said.

After Marty left, Rocky got in the Explorer and went down toward the little town. Danny went back into the house, where his mother was pouring another little glass of Jack Daniels.

"So what's he goin' to do with the money?" he asked. "Two hundred fifteen dollars."

"Oh, he's just getting a couple cartons of cigarettes and some drinks," she said. "So how's the situation with school? You've missed a lot."

"School's fine. Cartons of cigarettes cost forty-five bucks. That's ninety. Drinks go another thirty, right? We have to eat. We can't pay the electric bill."

"Oh, we'll figure that out," she said. The wet-lipped mellowness of her bearing irritated him. She didn't seem to care.

"When?"

"Oh now," she said. "Don't worry about it, okay?"

"Somebody's gotta."

"Look, let's wait until he comes back with the cigarettes, okay? I can't worry about this now. Let's just wait."

"And this stuff about selling this place? That's stupid. All he wants is whatever money it gets so he can—do what? I don't believe for a minute that he's starting up some business. That's bullshit."

"You're being belligerent," she said. "That's not like you."

"Becky told me."

"Told you what?" She looked up at him with vague perplexity.

"The picnic. Colorado, or whatever town it was. You know, what an honor it would be."

"I don't know what you're talking about."

"She told me."

"Well, she's made something up," she said. "I don't know why, but for some reason people seem to want to cut down this thing Rocky and I have going. I'll go ahead and let you do that—" She shook her head, then nodded as if she'd figured something out. "I'll let you do that, but I don't know why it is that I'm being prevented from just being happy. You try to surface and you get slapped in the face. I don't like it, I'll tell you, but I won't complain. Just go on, keep cutting."

"Okay," he said.

"We can't surface when we're being slapped in the face."

"Okay, sorry."


Rocky came back with the cigarettes and three bottles of booze. He said nothing about any change, and Danny waited for the right time to ask him. But as the day wore on, it seemed that there wasn't any right time. Rocky and his mother sat in the kitchen and talked, and drank. When the bus pulled up in the driveway and the kids came out, they saw the Explorer and, from the front window, he could tell that they were excited about it. Then there was all the greeting and how ya doin' stuff in the kitchen, and he waited in the living room, looking out the side window at the Explorer. It didn't take a genius to figure that they didn't have any nineteen thousand dollars, which meant that Rocky'd stolen the car. And it didn't take a genius to figure that any money they could make cutting logs would go where Rocky wanted it to go. And now, the conversation went on to Becky's tooth—he could hear his mother talking about it, and then Rocky. It didn't take a genius to figure out that the hundred dollars he had to fix her tooth would go the way of all the other money. He stood there looking at the dusted windowpane, its old, rippled glass warping the shape of the car, and thought, there isn't anything anybody can do about it. Can't be helped.

He went into the kitchen.

"Hey, can't they bill you?" Rocky asked.

"I don't think so, less you have a credit card."

"We were thinking," his mother said. "We thought we'd go to Otsego Lake on the weekend and rent a boat."

"Sure," he said. "That'd be fun."

"But we haven't got the money. We thought we'd have the filling billed to us and pay it later."

"So you want the money."

"Oh stop," his mother said. "Jeez, you'd think—"

"You runnin' the show now?" Rocky asked. "You the resident bean-counter?"

"Look," he said, "I paid the taxes, I bought the food, okay? You weren't here and you didn't send any money."

"I wanna go to Otsego," Becky said.

"Me too," Ron said.

"See?" Rocky said. "You've been out-voted." He turned to Becky. "You put on one of them skimpy bathing suits and wow all the rich boys in Cooperstown."

Danny took out his wallet, and took the hundred dollars he had folded in there, and gave it to his mother. "Not my tooth," he said.

"Lighten up," Rocky said.

"Okay." He turned to go back to the living room. Then he turned back. "So is there any point in my cutting logs any more?"

"What kind of a question is that?" Rocky asked. He looked at Danny's mother. "What the hell is this? Your boy's got a real mouth, I'll tell you." He turned back to Danny. "You got to clean up your act, kid. Here we been back two goddam hours and we hafta listen to this. Just clean it up, okay?"

Danny turned and went into the living room, amazed at what he'd heard. He had to clean up his act.


By later in the night, things were sort of jolly, with Rocky and his mother laughing it up in the kitchen, the kids all hopped up because Rocky told them he was buying a VCR-DVD machine so that they could rent movies. And by bedtime the jolliness carried over to Rocky's tickling Becky when they went in to say goodnight, his mother there saying, "Oh now, let's stop playing now," and Becky squealing, and Rocky saying, "Love to be the lucky guy! Love to be the lucky guy!" And then there was some discussion about playing so rough, Rocky doing the "Aww, come on now, it's just playin' around." Danny sat at his desk, listening, and then listening later as Rocky and his mother continued their boisterous talk in the kitchen.

In the morning there was no sign of them. It was apparent that they were sleeping in. Danny sat with the kids in the kitchen as they waited for the bus. When Ron went to the bathroom, Becky looked at Danny and said, "You know, I'd like to go stay at Martina's. This isn't workin' right."

"I know. I'll ask Ma when she gets up."

After the bus came and the kids left, he sat at the kitchen table and drank instant coffee, and waited. When it became apparent that they weren't planning on getting up by eight, he got his stuff together and went down to the woods. This time he would cut stovewood, and pulpwood, because he didn't want ash trees wasted on them, and he didn't want to squander the best wood they had. It was like a savings account. The longer you left them the bigger they got. He worked until he felt hungry enough for lunch and went back up the hill to the house. They were just getting up, it seemed, Rocky heating water for instant coffee and, just as Danny opened the kitchen door, pulling the Jack Daniels out of the cupboard. When he saw Danny he put it back. "So, you didn't go to school today, eh?" he said

"Nope. Gotta cut wood."

"Might as well cut it," Rocky said. "I'm lookin' into this Strout Realty thing. Been thinkin' that this place oughtta bring some bucks."

"You were gonna sell the car, right?"

"Thinkin' of it," he said, "if that's any of your business."

"Now," his mother said, "let's not start."

"I'm not starting anything," Danny said. "I was just wonderin'."

"Well, don't question what I'm doin', okay?"

"Okay." He turned to his mother. "Becky wants to stay with that friend of hers, Martina. They're doin' some project on Middle Eastern Religion, and—"

"When we just got back?" Rocky said. "Out of the question."

"Yeah, but—"

"Danny," his mother said, "it isn't the right time, okay? We just got back, and when she does that, she comes back with this—" She waved her hand around, shaking her head. "This attitude. It's like she's embarrassed about us, and she comes back with this attitude."

"Okay," Danny said. "She just asked me to ask you, that's all. Up to you."

"It's not that I don't want her to have friends. It's just that sometimes you end up feeling kind of like humiliated? I know that sounds funny to you, but it's the way people always looked down at us. I don't like it."

"Okay."

"I'll talk to her."

"I don't like it either," Rocky said. "Been goin' through that all my life."

Danny's mother nodded. "While we're trying to come up, to surface, we don't need any of that. Not now." She sighed, and shook her head. "There's always something that stands in your way."


Pulpwood. He looked for trees that had no symmetry, that were thinner in the trunk, ones that he couldn't see growing into good logs. Make a chip with the measuring stick, forty and some inches. In one spot, the stick was blackened by the grease and oil from his and his father's hands. It went back so many years that Danny couldn't remember. By the time he got a good load, it was around one o'clock, and he hauled it up the hill to the dock. It wasn't enough—he'd have to cut at least two more cords to satisfy Marty Wallace. Looking at the house, he saw that the Explorer wasn't there.

His mother sat in the kitchen and looked a little bleary. She watched him as he went to the pot for coffee water. While he was stirring the instant coffee, he cleared his throat and said, "Look, I don't think it's a good idea to sell this place. It's all we got, and we can make good money cutting logs."

"Keepin' it's not an option," she said.

"Why?"

"Don't do this, okay?"

"Okay, but we gotta figure this out sometime. I mean, a whole load of logs went down the tubes. I don't know what to do about that."

"There's nothing we do about it," she said. "We have to live."

"So, did he steal the Explorer?"

The look on her face started as an outraged disbelief in what he said, and then changed to a strange, dismissive fatigue. She sighed, and then laughed. "Can you imagine it? Some stupid fool parks the car at a gas station where Rocky's buying beer, leaves the motor running with the keys inside, and goes to the men's room. Kept it running for the air conditioning I guess. So what's Rocky supposed to do? He sees the key in there, figures the door's open. The dumb idiot who went into the men's room is still in there? What is he supposed to do?"

"I don't know."

"Sure," she said, drawing the word out. "Sure, leave it where it is. Sure. I mean, here's this ridiculous situation, a man so stupid that he doesn't even deserve to have a good car in the first place, leaves it like that. You're standing there looking at this car and you know how cool it is inside? What can you do?" Then she looked up at him with apparent surprise, as if she did not believe what she had just said. "Now wait," she said. "This is just between us. You say nothing about this, do you understand?"

"Okay."

"It'd ruin everything. Everything we're working for. You say anything and it's over, don't you see?" She shook her head, staring at the table with wonder. "It would be the end of us, of me. I'd die."

"So what about Becky? What do we do about that?"

"We said, just get the tooth filled and have them bill us."

"No, I mean what about him? What about what he—"

"Oh boy," she said, shaking her head. "Here we go. You have this misunderstanding, and you can't let go of it. Really, you've got to let go of it, okay?"

"I'm not sure it's a misunderstanding."

Her eyes began to glaze a little, in a preface to crying. He waved his hands at her. "I take it back."

"We're doing what we can," she moaned. "We're trying the best way we can."

"Okay."

He heard the Explorer coming in the driveway. The door slammed, but Rocky did not come in. Danny went to the window. Rocky had walked down to the road to examine the load of pulpwood. He took his hat off and stood there, and shook his head, apparently laughing.

Danny went outside, and walked past the Explorer, touching the side of it as he walked. When he got to the road, Rocky turned.

"You gotta be kidding me," he said. "Pulpwood? What the fuck is this?"

"It's pulpwood."

"You asshole," Rocky said, putting his cap back on. "You come up with pulpwood? Ash trees all over the place and you come up with this?"

Danny looked at the load, and then felt shaky and weak in the knees. It felt like anger and shame mixed, that airy hollowness in which he didn't know what to think, or how to respond. He looked at Rocky, and said, "Savin' ash for like a bank account."

Rocky laughed with a kind of irritated astonishment. "Stupid idiot," he said. "They ain't no use standin' where they are. You got a fucking brain in your head? Ash, for chrissakes. Get the ash. Don't you see what we're doin' here?"

That airy hollowness was still there, but now Danny felt his heart thumping in his chest, because the logic of what he understood now was so forceful and so obvious that the next thing was as if done already, as if he were in mid-air after jumping off something and couldn't go back.

"It's not yours to sell. It's my mom's and dad's."

"She can't do for herself," he said. "That's my job."

"I don't wanna sell it."

"You got nothin' to say in this you little asshole, nothin'."

"And then there's my sister."

Rocky screwed his face up at him. Then he sneered, as if an idea had come to him. "Which one?" he asked, and laughed. "Huh? Which one?" Then he nodded brightly, as if expecting Danny to get the joke.

"No, I'm talking about that stuff about the little town in Colorado or whatever and what an honor it would be. I'm talkin' about Becky and what you're after. You gotta keep your hands off her." Rocky moved closer, and Danny lapsed further into the sensation of light, airy nothingness.

"Who the fuck are you?" Rocky asked, his face now only a couple of feet from Danny's. "You candy-assed little jerk. Huh?" He poked Danny in the chest. "Who are you?"

"No," he said. "It's you. You're the problem here. You're gonna keep your hands—"

His head snapped back in a sickening, silver flash, and the impact of his buttocks on the hard dirt rattled up his spine and he bruised the heels of his hands. He sat up, opening his mouth to speak, and a hard shot to the hollow inside his shoulder snapped his body around. Lying on his elbow, he realized that the last one was a kick. "Listen," he said, and felt bubbling at his nose. It was bleeding.

"Don't fuck with me," the voice above him said, and then he heard the crunching of Rocky walking across the dirt road to the driveway.

He stayed there on his elbow for a few minutes, holding his nose. When he tried to stand, the pain shot out of his shoulder, and his arm felt numb, and he couldn't lift it.

He went up the drive slowly, holding his nose. Vaguely he was aware that his mother had appeared on the porch.

"Oh my God," she said. "Oh my God. Danny, come in here and let me—"

"...'m all right," he said.

"Danny, what happened? You sassed him. Oh my God, you can't do that."

"Did it," he said, making his way past her.

"I'll get ice," she said.

"Don't need ice." He didn't see Rocky, and then heard sounds from the bathroom.

In his room he found a white sock and held it under his nose. His shoulder hurt badly, and he worried that something had gone wrong there. He got a pencil stub and a little slip of paper and went to the window, and his hand shaking so ridiculously that he could barely write, he took down the Explorer's license plate number. Then he went back downstairs and to the kitchen. His mother looked up at him.

"Are you all right?" she asked.

"Yeah," he said, and hearing Rocky come out of the bathroom, he went outside.

He found that if he jammed his left hand under his belt, his arm didn't jog and hurt as much. When he had gone five hundred yards, he considered going crosslots to the road that led to the town and the school, but wasn't sure he wanted to climb through fences, so he walked, and kept walking in a dreamlike, mesmerized, gait, holding the sock under his nose and keeping his hand jammed under his belt. When he got to the dirt road that turned and went to the blacktop road to town, he turned, and just as he did so he heard a vehicle behind him. It was the Explorer. He went into the woods. Standing inside the woods, he waited for the car to pass, but it turned onto the road and stopped about fifty yards ahead of where he stood off the road. He could see Rocky looking around.

"C'mon kid!" he called. "Cut the shit and let's go home." He walked along the road. "You push this and your ma'll end up in the funny farm, kid. You'll pay for it, I guarantee you." In the distance Danny heard the sound of the bus.

He waited. Rocky stood there, apparently listening, and then got in the Explorer, turned it around, and drove back the way he had come.

He got a ride on the back of a flatbed with three men in it, the driver saying to him, "Yup, you better get yourself over to a doctor, boy. What, a cow kicked ya did it?"

"Fell," Danny said. His nose bled as he released the sock to pull himself up on the truck bed, and the effort of doing that shot pain through his shoulder that radiated into his chest and down to his hand.

They dropped him off at the school. He half hoped that no one would be there, but could see the principal's car, the school nurse's car, and other cars in the side parking lot.

He took a deep breath, and went over in his mind what he had: sexual harassment was it? Or was it pedophile stuff? Then what? Assault. And finally car theft, which he assumed any cop with a computer could verify. He went to the steps and stopped, and tried peeking inside his shirt. His shoulder was blue, with a bad scrape on the inside. His nose was still trickling blood. Oh, how they were going to hate him now. No VCR-DVD, no Otsego Lake. He felt himself moving toward the impulse to cry, and fought it off. They would never forgive him.

Opening the door and walking into the hall, which had become strangely unfamiliar to him now, as if he were walking into a building he had never been in before, he thought that if he had hated himself before, for one thing or another, he was surely going to hate himself now.

# A Story of Water
# You Could Never Tell

S its there watching the warrior princess with green eyes—she does a flip in mid-air and smashes her foot into the face of a guy in leather whose sword falls into a ravine.

"Dad."

"Wait."

Wheels a foot up into another clod's face, then stands over him, her ample chest heaving out of a tight leather vest studded with metal buttons. The clod on the ground groans, confusion on his bleary-eyed, unshaven face.

"I need money for the gas."

Struggling in his jeans, pulls out two greasy dollar bills. How the hell could he just get back and have no gas left? Holding out the money, "No videos. Wrestlin's on tonight."

No money to rent one anyway, so it's beefy steroid pumped guys with spiked hair and tattoos. Take the money. So it's walk six miles, but then walking's all right.

Stop at the kitchen and peek back in. While the warrior princess rides off breasts bouncing, long thighs sliding on her horse, he reaches into the crack by the cushion and brings out the can of beer, takes a sip. Least he hides it until noon.

Dusty gas can in the woodshed, and it's out, the can bonging once from air pressure after the sun hits it, and it's around the house toward the road where the huge splintered loading dock sits piled with pulpwood. Along the house, past the window of the corner room—look in through the dusty window and there's the bed, and why the hell he keeps that bed, like a high cot, metal piping and a gear mechanism, when she died what was it? Four, no five years ago now. And the light string with the little metal bell shaped thing on the bottom—used to punch it away again and again while standing there talking to her, punch away and back it came, until he yelled, Cut that out! and she said, It's all right. He's a boy. Let him—

Eight-thirty maybe. Don't like the long walk but do, because it's all like humming quiet with the funny rush of thinking all around. It'll be past Evan Wright's house all collapsed into its foundation and then the Roberts' house empty with broken windows, and barns fallen down. Except for old John Moore who takes a half an hour to walk to his mailbox every day. Hell, could be dead too and just not know it. Kind of embarrassed about walking past what's left alive here though—the Washburn house because Mrs. Washburn is dying of cancer there and you just have to go past, and Caroline Washburn, the spike-haired white-faced black-lipped punk rocker goes to school each day with her mother there dying, and at school if you look at her, her eyes say one word and I'll rip your face off, and off she walks with her punk friends. Was before summer though. Now, stays home to watch her mother die.

Clop clop. Uh-oh. She stands in the middle of the road on the grass strip bisecting the dirt tracks. She looks, chewing. Shit. Gotta go back. Don't go back and she'll clop clop all the way to town in that sleepy flouncing cow walk.

Leave the can. She watches—don't scare her any more because she's too old, what? nineteen maybe. Get close and she raises her head. "Go home. I already milked you, you old fart."

She chews, and there is a long low churning grumble in her belly, and she listens to it, thinking, and then burps, and a blast of warm, sweet, fermented air like the air in a silo billows up. Her eyes are huge and dewey, like black liquid wells, her ears soft and oily. "G'wan home." Nothing. "C'mon, I'll give you grain later," and pick out and share the molasses bullets with her, taste good those things, almost like candy, all the way back to when Billy and Stu and Eveline were here and when there were cows in the pasture and when she was alive before there was that goddam gear-bed.

Clap hands, a mild alarm crosses her face, and she turns half way. Slap rump, and clop clop off she goes, bag swinging.

Back to the can, sitting tipped on the center grass. Then it's along through a kind of tunnel, sun-dappled through the leaves overhead, and down a little past the swamp, dragonflies glinting above the water, which gathers at the hilltop near Evan Wright's foundation with its rose bushes still growing by the porch, and then the water forms the little stream that runs all the way down to town. Where it's narrow enough to jump across it's deep, the black shadows of trout moving two, three feet down.

The night she died she called, three, four in the morning. Up, and to the stairs, grumbling and groggy, feeling your way through the blackness. What? Could you get me a glass of water? and you went partway down and slipped, banged your ankle, cursed. No, go back, never mind.

It's okay.

Go back, never mind.

And so it was back and she died before dawn and it's something only you know and can never tell anybody, because it was only a glass of water she wanted and you went back and she was dead in the morning. Nobody knows. There is a blackness inside right at the center that nobody can ever know. Can never be thirsty without remembering.

The hilltop beyond the Roberts house comes into view bobbing with the walking, the pastures and woods all sloping down, the picture bisected by the bright green hummocks that bank the little stream, and the tan dirt road next to it. Shimmering in the distance, boiled by the heat off the road, is Caroline Washburn's house, and walking past it will make a funny embarrassed buzz because Mrs. Washburn is dying, maybe dead already, and walking past, the eyes in the window will say, you walking past the house, my mother is dying, my wife is dying—why don't you look or wave or something? So just grit the teeth and walk. All mothers die. And when she did there was nothing, with him drinking in the house and there was no place to go to sort of feel complete except the workbench in the barn because of the hollow dusty silence and the way the sunlight hit the wood and tools and cans through the gaps in the old wall, a series of lines like bars so bright and dense with color that it made the snow all around less white. And he sat drinking in the house.

The rhythm of walking settles—every hundred yards the sweaty handle of the can goes to the other side, the side of the can bonged once by the knee as it passes. The brook hisses next to the road.

Then the Washburns' house bobs in the vision, a light on in the kitchen, the huge brown silo glinting. Look straight ahead at the bluish haze the trees make, eat up the road each step, knees and feet shooting out.

Smoke. Why? In a clump of trees by the brook across from the house. Is that fire? Another little billow rises, spreads like dream wings on the air and vanishes.

Step to the roadside and look.

Uh-oh. Caroline Washburn. Sitting on a tree root smoking a cigarette and then kerplunking pebbles into the water, her hair spiked and orange, her black leather jacket and black leather jeans studded with silver, a thick silver chain across one hip. Her lips are black like in school, face almost paper white, like what is that stuff they put on?

Sees you.

"Hey." What to say? So look around, trees, pasture, road. "Y'know, there's trout in there."

"Like, I'm so impressed I could puke."

So say, "Yeah, well," and look around. Trees, pasture, road. "Goin' to get some gas." Everybody with nothing to say says yeah, well.

Says, "So go." Black fingernails too, and hey, black toes. Wearing sandals she is—not the heavy black shoes of school, and the hair, the color of orange juice almost. Brown once.

So go, then stop. "How's your—" Can't even use the word 'mother.' "Your ma?"

"Half dead. Why?"

"Just wonderin'."

"Don't like to see me smoke so I come here."

"Yeah." Flat look on her face. "Well." And why does she wear that shit at home? "Hey, lemme just take a look in the water."

Shrugs. Do whatever rings your gong. Got a little tape player and tapes. What? The skinny creep formerly known? Kiss? Nirvana?

Go down the bank. Can't see her house from here. Sits right by a deeper pool, almost black it is like a cow's eye with trout hiding in the bottom. Kerplunking more pebbles.

"This is a real clean stream. I know the beginning of it, up by our house."

Snort. Like, big fucking deal her face says. And the black leather jeans so tight it looks like it must hurt.

"Well, gotta go."

"Really."

Up to the road.

Her voice behind, "Hey, on your way back, stop. I'll show you something cool. I mean like, really cool."

"...'kay."

The road goes off diminished to a blueblack haze in the trees. It's maybe a hundred yards, and then the can goes from one hand—bong—to the other. From here it's two miles to the hard road.


Only a gallon but it gets heavy even though gasoline weighs less than water, and Curt Steele said hey, hang around a while and I'll give you a ride, and it was, nah, it's okay. Because she had something cool to show, and the can goes from one hand to the other every hundred feet now, sloshing and bonging deep and the can like drawing breath in the sun and wheezing with little bubbles around the cap, and it's all up, up the hard road that looks like a long strip of frayed black electrical tape holding the pastures and hayfields down, like tape on pillows almost, and then it's into the dirt road that for the first mile is a cool tunnel through the trees.

Stop. A sound, kind of tickling from just under the beginning of hearing. Coming from all directions or— No. Ahead. It's music—sound in the woods doesn't go in a line but radiates out and then comes at you from the side or behind, like it coils around things. Hey, not music really but rap. Then a squeak, something else. Then it's whatsername—like a prayer.

Down in the same place on a hummock kerplunking pebbles.

"Hey."

Turns, then pushes one of those square buttons on the tape machine. Silence, like that hushed whooshing in the trees.

Looks up. "You got a CD player?"

"No."

"All the kids at school do."

Because they're town kids. They have TVs in their rooms too, and cars. Worst is they have running water and not outhouses but bathrooms, and where do boys go for their outhouse dreams then? They have parents who work wearing suits who go to PTA and complain about bad influences and belong to DARE and MADD and— What do folks here belong to? SHIT. Stupid Hicks in—

"C'mon."

Leave the can. Follow her along the brook. Stupid Hicks In. Jeans so tight it's got to hurt, like they're painted on and each cheek is like black skin glinting in the indentations with each step.  Outhouse dreams.  Town boys would do it in the shower.

Trees.  Trouble.  T.

The brook divides.  "Hey."

"What?"  Turns.

"It branches here.  I never knew that."

"Goes back just down a ways."

Like her face is so white.  Black lipstick makes it whiter.

"Then technically we're on an island."

Snorts, stops, hands on her black hips.  Says, "Wow, I'm like—  I mean I'm like speechless."

"Yeah, well—"

So what is it?  Stops, stands by a weed in a little clearing out of sight of the house.  "Look."

"Is it some kind of a flower?"

Sighs at the sky, shakes her head.  "Duh, it's pot."

"Really?"  So look—bright green sawtooth leaves, then a dense gathering of them at the ends of the little branches.

"Somebody gave me a seed.  Hey, I dropped it in the hall at school and it bounced like a high-bouncer or a bee-bee.  Like I'm all running around chasing it and Mr. Valentine sees me and I'm all, 'It's a candy!  It's a candy!' and he's all glaring at me—"  In the patch of sunlight her moving lips move more because they are black, the little vertical lines showing natural lip through.  "—so I stuck it in here a month ago and blam—dope."

Nod.  "Yeah."  So it's pot.  "Well—"

"Whaddaya doin' tomorrow?"

"Pulpwood.  All week.  My dad's back is bad—gets his disability check though.  I do the cutting except on Sunday."  And he won't watch sports.  Only warrior princesses and girls in spandex doing aerobics, and war movies.  No basketball.

"C'mon down and we can get high."

"It puts holes in your brain I heard."

"Who cares?"  Reaches in and breaks off a branch and the weed shudders.  "We dry this and roll a joint next week.  Whoah, this is sticky."

Your mother is dying, did you remember that?

"Okay."  Won't really do it.  "I better get on."

"We always wondered why you guys live on that hill. We used to see your car parked at the bottom in winter."

"Yeah."  Well—  And it was wintertime when she died. And he had a hard time of it, but made his way away from the hard booze to beer and now he's all right.  "Old days I guess horses didn't spin their wheels.  I mean—"

Laughs.  "That's cool.  Horses with wheels."

"I better get on."  Was so much walking then, even the tractor wouldn't go through that snow.

Along the brook, up there the can sits red on the hummock.  Behind, she is saying something, "—inside a regular cigarette paper.  I'll show you."

"Okay."

And then the road goes all the way up over the hill, then another, and then up, and the can will get heavy. And it was winter when she died, when she asked for the water, and it was no, never mind.  Never mind.  It's the black secret you could never let anybody know.  Like a short snake resting inside the front of the backbone, from neck to guts it sits there kind of dense and oily so you can feel it, separate from other organs but sliding on them when you walk, the can wheezing in the sun.

A bluish haze hangs in the woods, the electric buzz of insects everywhere, and she holds the empty filter cigarette up, drops in little flakes of it, and then carefully slides a twig down the paper tube and tamps, her black lower lip held between her teeth.

"Does the filter filter out the dope?"

"Nope."

"You ever done this before?"

Holds her lip in her teeth, tamping, and the black leather jeans strain against her thighs and buttocks. An outhouse dream for sure, and wonder if Billy and Stu did it too in the outhouse. Sure they did. They were boys. But funny, here with her, a living breathing girl sort of what? Like glowing with something, makes a rush in the chest all the way down and around the low stomach, and nobody around and there she is tamping pot into a tube of paper. Like the whole idea of it is so tangible with her tamping pot with her girl's parts and not six feet away from you with your boy's parts and it is like water to a—

Says, "You come next Sunday, help me do some body piercing."

"Huh?"

"I'll get a cork and needle and alcohol. Nose maybe."

"No way."

Tamps, squinting. This close up can see the make-up, like a thin layer of caulk or maybe plaster. Alone—like there's a real girl under there. School, she passes by and Bob Cable says, look at the ass on her, and it's just laughing, and you see her in the hall and her eyes are flat, challenging, and she goes off and Bob or Steve or Rick says, I'd like to get a little of that. In school it's a distance. But real flesh girl or not, her mother is dying.

"How's your—"

Nothing. Then, "I'm like not interested in talking about that now, okay?"

"How's your dad take it?"

"Stays like a little drunk most of the time."

The stream gurgles. On the island. It's sound from both sides, inside the electric buzz of insects. And it's like remember not to say anything bad before you leave in case he dies before you get back. No more black snakes.

"...'kay, let's get high."

Lights it like a regular cigarette, then holds some smoke in her lungs. Hands it over. Smoked only a few times, so just don't cough and make a jerk out of yourself is all.

It's a sweet, acrid, thick, almost oily smoke somewhere between timothy stalks, salt and molasses. Let it out.

Black lips move. "Feel anything yet?"

"No."

Giggles. "Then when we're high we're supposed to have sex, right?"

"Yeah—" Well. Look around. She's nuts, that's what it is. She's off her rocker. It's no wonder why they talk about her at school. But she's got to be kidding—they would never do like that. And then there's that ticklish rush again, like even takes the breath away, her all moving and alive like that.

Takes another puff, hands it over. Black lipstick on the tan filter. More timothy, salt and molasses. Hold it until the dizzy inflation is almost too much. Let it out.

Black lips move. "Know what a rave is?"

"No."

"It's kind of like a rock orgy with drugs and sex and yelling and screaming and smoke. Herbal ecstasy and coke, ice and angel dust."

"Yeah."

"And where's the nearest one?"

Bright, kind of happy, her face.

Says, "What? Fifty miles? Doesn't that suck? I wanna be like super mega bad but like, who the hell would even know? I mean I could dress any way I wanted. Only the cows and chipmunks would know."

Raises her hand for another puff and there's an image left for each inch going up, like fingers waved before a TV screen, the transparent forearms and hands trailing the real one and vanishing one by one in place. "Jeez." And she's flat, two-dimensional, and behind her the trees pulse and the whisper of them comes toward so that hearing is seen as a kind of spiral coming, and then her voice is flat like an old radio two rooms away speaking in a foreign language. A long empty tumbling sigh and the ground moves underneath. Sit down. Thump.

Some time passes, what? An hour? It's the water is what it is, saying something in a soft whisper.

Laughing, she is. And the long coil of sound comes from the trees in a winding spiraled pulse, and she laughs at you, talks, and the ridicule and hatred in her voice is so that the only thing to do is feel the empty ticklish yawn moving and like leaving the ghost of flesh behind. Your mother is dying, you know. Did you remember that?

Not there. So, where'd she go? Rise up, the plane of trees shifting, their sound coiling out. Turn, the woods dance. Can't hear any more, only the pulsing rush of blood in the ears, whoosh whoosh whoosh. Where is she? Okay, by the brook. Turn again and there she is, standing there, her face a strange flat white mask of what? She's scared, holding her fists under her chin. "What?" Can't really talk right. She backs up shaking her head no no no no no as if to say why are you here when my mother is dying? Turn, and then almost like dipping into molten metal the foot is in the water to the knee, silt ballooning up then sweeping downstream in a fat arrow with a point vanishing into an eddy.

Her face said go away. Walking feels empty, like floating on up the road, the water squishing in the sneaker. Like burning, the water, like it melted the calf right off down to clean bone. Like it was molten silver and on the road it's walking on the grass strip in the middle. At night when there were no stars it was blind black and you walked on the grass strip in the middle to know where you were, walked all the way up and walked until in the distance there would be the light in her room at the corner of the house.

Wait until an ad, because the warrior princess is going to have a big fight with a blonde princess in leather with breasts as big as hers or bigger. So it's a flying hamburger now and onions and tomato slices dancing with bright drops of water in slow motion and, "Like I said, it was Wednesday when I took the load to the hardroad dock. The wreath was on the door that day."

Looks halfway up and in the chair-crack the beercan pops softly. "Means she died Tuesday maybe."

"I mean like should we take a box of canned goods like people did when—"

And remember that. A knock on the door and Mrs. Moore handed the box in—soup and Dinty Moore Beef Stew and soda.

Eyes still on the TV, "I ain't seen Bob Washburn in a while. 'sides, I saw cars there Thursday. They got plenty of family. Don't worry about it."

"Yeah, well—"

"Don't worry about it."

The warrior princess'll be back soon. They're going to go at it on a cliff above a raging river.

Out. So what now? She said come Sunday but can't, really, because her mother died, and they will have to bury her. Somewhere like the town cemetery maybe. And remember that. The casket going down in those straps, and saying nothing. And saying nothing at home, him sitting in front of the TV and the only place to go the bench in the barn to look at the bars of light through billows of breath vapor. Like saying nothing for a month but I cooked up a can of beans, you want some? and him looking at the TV and saying sure. And for a long time it was standing at the bench because of the silence and the bars of light.

So it's to the road? Maybe they buried her already. Pass the corner of the house and look in through finger-print-cleared holes at the crank-bed. Superimposed there is a still image of an emaciated woman's profile, hands on the cover like dried pale roots. Could at least walk past just to see. Then what?

The tan tire depressions sweep away parallel, to a point where against the blueblack hollow under the trees they converge. Not a lazy walk either, more like a march, but what the hell can you do? It's only proper to at least show up no matter what because she said it, before all of that other went wrong and her face said go away, my mother is dying.

No clop clop. Where is she now? Off down the hill to the west a long sweeping hayfield to a huge maple tree next to which is a spring that comes up into a steel cone, the lump of water dancing. She's there, a broadside profile almost as if she set herself that way to say, here I am, long's you milk me and give me grain I'll do what you say. So it's walk.

Evan Wright. His house gray splintered planking and burdock bushes, roses. And the Roberts house sagging with its broken windows. And John Moore—how long will there be smoke curling from that chimney? Like it's everybody dies and nothing gets left alive behind.

Out of the cool tunnel and down the hill, and off there in the distance the house and the brown silo. No cars. Go anyway. Where do you put a road? If it's next to a stream then you put it on only one side unless you want to build a bridge.

Nobody there. Jog down the bank to the kerplunking hummock. Well, so it's maybe a couple of pebbles and off home. Showed up at least. Kerplunk.

Scrapes of leather on dirt, and down she comes, her hair pink now, dayglow pink, lipstick like blueblack, and green finger and toenails.

"Hey."

"Hey."

Looks around. "Where'd you go last week?"

"Home? You told me to go?"

"It was what they call a bad trip. After you left I barfed my guts out."

Stands there, funny look of breath held or a question not quite asked, breeze ruffling pink hair.

"Sorry about your—"

Nods. "Tuesday, like noon or something. We—" Stops. Face changed now, shaking her head. "I can't—I mean—"

"Yeah, well—"

"C'mon."

On the island.  Same black leather jeans like painted on, moving with each step and glinting dully in planes and then flashing lines.  But not an outhouse dream now.  Her mother died.  Under the tree she sits, the water hissing behind her.  Reaches in her jacket and brings out what?  Vodka.

"We'll get high on this."

"Okay."

"Besides, I want to get a buzz on before the piercing."

Takes a little sip, looks into the middle distance at nothing, swallows.  Then her face twists up.  "God that burns."

Holds the flask out.  Take a sip, down it goes into a strange, expanding burn that feels like a slow pumping of hot pressure out and into the neck and cheeks.  The eyes expand into overinflated balls.

Takes stuff out—a little bottle, a what?  Sewing needle with a thread, a cork, a ring, no, an earring that looks like a ring.

Another sip, and, "I put this inside my nose and you poke the needle through, okay?  Like, I can't do it.  Then we put this alcohol on the hole and put the ring in."

"The cork is too big."

Looks at it.

"What about the ring?  Isn't that too big?"

Staring at the ring.

"I mean how do you blow your nose and all?"

"Nipple then.  Or belly button."

No way.

Looks up.  Something strange on her face, so white, like a mask caught without anybody knowing what it was supposed to show.  "Goddam chicken.  I'll do it myself. The nipple."

Flush. "But who would you show it to?" Don't do it here. No way. "I mean a ring that big has to go somewhere. Even on a belly button it would—"

Takes another sip of vodka, hands it over. Lost now. Listening to something, like insects or hissing water, the cork held up, the needle and ring bright on her thigh. Like sounds only she hears, from the side.

Sip, and it goes down and radiates like furnace heat.

"You could get an infection."

Looks now, right at the eyes so you have to look away.

"I mean some like qualified guy should do that. How do you know—"

"Go home." Looks at the cork, thinking. Drops it in the water and it dances in an eddy, then rises up over a hill of flowing dark water and zip it's gone, down to town. Throws the needle and the ring in the water, the little bottle next, and off it goes bobbing down to town.

"I was in her room all like arguing with her and she asked me if I ever did it with a boy and I told her I did cause I wanted to be bad." Hands under her chin now, like two posts holding her head up because she is shaking. "Then she died. I mean I lied to her and then she— She—"

Should go. Get away. This is her thing and she shouldn't be saying this. "Yeah, well—"

Moves on her buttocks to the water, and shaking too, like stung by something, eyes wide with seeing something so awful that you want to close them but can't.

"Look, I gotta go."

The face turns, one look of a kind of hatred that says, so go already. Turns back and puts her hands in the water and cups it, then up to her face, shoulders shaking while she wipes, the water running down off her jacket like skim milk, and the white melts away, the lipstick too, and she turns, her face wet, and says, "She—" Can't say it.

"Look, I gotta—"

"She didn't like me."

"Yeah, but—"

"She died and she didn't like me."

Nervous. This stuff is not anybody's business but hers, and she looks, like you could say something. Then she moves close, freckles on her face under the pink hair, and leans, shoulder against your chest so that the smell of pink hair and water and leather roils up, and there is no way to move or get away. She rolls up into a ball and starts to cry.

"She died and she didn't like me."

Road's only fifty or sixty yards away. Stuck though. So put one arm around her shoulders. Like that maybe, and she moves, tightening herself into a ball. So pat her a little? Oops, not there but up a little.

"She did like you. She just—"

Shakes her head, moans a high pitched sound that melts into the trees. "No she didn't." She sits away a little, looks at the water. "Go away. Forget it."

Sit. So okay, never mind. Road's only right there. The water sweeps by, long strands of grass waving in it at the edges, and it's like, maybe get up now and go, but there is a little thump in the chest, like a bump when it comes clear what was in the head before there was any way of knowing it was there.

"Can I tell you something?"

Nods at the water, looking away, so it's talk at the back of her head right there fifteen inches away.

"I mean I know what you said because of something that happened." That makes a flash of heat, a kind of shaky, awful cringe. The road's up there, so close.

Waits, listening, almost like relaxing into it, and can almost feel her waiting, and there is the smell of leather and the sweet smell of scalp and hair and the vapor of vodka and the radiating electricity, like the buzz you can feel next to anything alive.

"I mean what it is is about a glass of water."

Breathless almost, like it catches in the throat, but otherwise it would be only the huge buzzing silence all around. So you just fill it with something, go ahead with it, her and the trees and stream and everything waiting to hear.

# Fire Dance

The misshapen nails and ash white scars on the backs of his father's fingers were caused by a fire, which burned the family house when Philip Longley was only one. The fire took two victims, his brother and sister, and whenever Longley saw his father's hands, at ten, or seventeen, or now at twenty-six, he would conceive a death scene that he had been revising in his mind all his life, according to the nature of the imagination at whatever age he was. His father had tried to climb in a second-story window to rescue the two children, but the fire ate at his fingers until he fell.

Longley's brother and sister had remained enigmatic ghosts in his mind all his life, even though he grew up in a new house built where the old one had stood. He could never escape the fact of their shadows, and the sensation of their presence seemed to him almost as tangible as some inborn physical handicap. This, he figured, was the reason he wanted all the distance he could get from his home, both geographical and in terms of likeness to his own origins.

But he had to make the obligatory yearly visit, this time especially because his mother had died while Longley and his wife were off in Europe on a vacation delayed until two years after they were married. After they returned he had two weeks to fully absorb her death before going to visit his father, and at his old house, the lack of her presence seemed to become normal after two days. Longley found himself secretly itching to leave as soon as was proper. Being home inspired a condition of a kind of neurotic indolence that he couldn't stand. He ended up wandering from room to room, as if held in some nearly catatonic expectation to see something different, in the cellar, the bedrooms, or the gloomy disorder of the attic.

Another reason to escape was that his father was up to something obvious, with his tours of the place, his gravelly speeches about the land values and so on. He stressed particularly the new little shopping center across the road. Only two hundred yards away, it consisted of a supermarket on the left, and a line of small shops—drugstore, shoe store, auto parts store, and a health food store. Even though the old man hated the shopping center, Longley could tell that he was using it as a prime carrot, probably assuming that his business-major son and city-girl daughter-in-law would be most impressed by that. After a day of this Longley informed him that there was no likelihood that he would be coming back after college. He knew what the old man wanted, to fulfill some old-fashioned desire for handing down property, in this case three hundred acres of broken down dairy farm and fifty cows. The barn was all right and the milking equipment new, bulk tank stuff, but the atmosphere, the laughable remoteness of the region, even despite the large village the place was at the edge of, turned Longley off.

As for Noreen, her attitude about the place was no threat to Longley. To his relief she was totally out of place in the country. The last summer they visited, she walked around always with a little wrinkle on the bridge of her nose. It was the manure smell, which she claimed penetrated every fabric of the house, even her clothes. Her distaste was forcefully backed up one day when they wandered down the drive past the mangers, past the bony rumps of the cows all lined up in their stanchions with their tails swishing back and forth, keeping flies off their hides. He was telling her that the black and white ones, which made up most of the herd, were Holsteins, the typical upstate New York cow, and the little brown ones were Jerseys, and that they all knew which stanchions were theirs. As he explained how the piped milking system worked, a cow nearby lifted her tail, and as was usual in the summer, sent a deep green stream into the gutter. Just as Noreen had passed the cow, it coughed, sending the stream a full five feet across the drive and onto the skirt of one of her best dresses, and onto a pair of fifty-dollar shoes. Longley had laughed instinctively, remembering how that always happened, and she fled out of the barn, cursing furiously at the manure and equally at him. She had come from Long Island, and had never been that close to a cow before.

So Longley figured that with the old man's expectations dashed, it was time to tell him that they would leave soon, maybe in two days. There seemed nothing more to say about the death of his mother, and Longley wanted three more weeks of peace before the fall semester started. Sitting at the table on the third morning of the visit, he looked across at Noreen and said, "I'm going to tell him now. Where is he?"

"Outside, down by that tube that goes under the road," she said. "Listen, if the house that was here burned like that, why did he build this one on its place?"

"I don't know. I always thought it was funny. I mean strange."

"What did your mother say?"

"Not a thing. Nothing at all."

"Yesterday he said in a while we'd get to see a calf born. Two weeks maybe."

Longley sighed. "Too gory for you, I suspect. Besides, we'll be long gone."

She laughed. "No. I don't have the same reaction this time. I mean even the smell. I sort of understand it this time—you know, like fermented hay? I don't mind it really."

"Well," Longley said, and went out the door.

He found his father at the mouth of the huge, corrugated steel tube that ran under the two-lane highway. He was pulling tentatively at some of the thick branches and debris that had clogged it up last spring. "Now the goddam highway guys told me this would be—whatchacallit—'maintained'," he said. "Sure as hell don't look maintained to me. Look maintained to you?" Longley snorted. The tube was built to permit the old man's cows access to a pasture and pond cut off from them by the construction of the shopping center. The pasture was too small to be of any use to them, but they always needed the water late in the summer. When they built the center they had to install the tube free, because the wells on the Longleys' side of the road always went low in the summer. The piped system in the mangers went almost dry. And the drainage ditches beyond the shopping center were too deep for the cows to cross over the road.  Longley remembered how in spring there would be a muddy river running down from the mountain behind the house and barn, which would spread its debris in the field where they later built the center.

Longley went down the grassy bank, and grabbed the end of a thick branch, and they both pulled on it.  The other end, disappearing into the flat, dry silt in the bottom of the tube, didn't move.  Mr. Longley sighed and stood up straight, then groaned.

"Back?"

"Yeah."

"We can get the tractor, or the chainsaw."

"So what do you do with an MBA degree?  Do you do business administration?"

"Yeah, sort of.  Or I'll teach—college."

Longley climbed back up on the bank toward the wire fence that ran along the highway.  His father followed, once slipping and catching himself with his hands.  Longley didn't reach for his hand, as he thought he should.  Standing up, the old man said, "I called the turkeys three times." He looked across the highway at the little shopping center. "See off to the left there?"

Longley nodded.  "Yeah, I remember."

"Dumb place to put a supermarket," his father said. "A full mile out of town."

"It's taxes, and land rental—you know, costs.  So they put it out here."

"I knew I shoulda bought that goddam field twenty years ago."  He stared at the fence, thinking, and kicking in the dirt with the square tip of his workshoe.  "If they don't clean this up today, I'm cuttin' the fence.  Drive them right across that parking lot.  Cut the other wire."

"Can't.  Traffic."

"It's my wire."

Longley experienced a flash of imaginary mortification. The old man might do just that. All his life he had been embarrassed by his father's crudeness. He could be seen placing his knuckle against one nostril and snorting vigorously out the other in places like the parking lot of the town's best restaurant. When Longley was fifteen or sixteen, his father would appear at school functions smelling slightly of beer and dressed like a comic bumpkin from a movie. And now, even with the distance Longley had achieved, he could still feel flashes of heat in his face when he thought of the old man's skirmishes with the town maintenance department, who would not clean the tube, and the shopping center people, who considered the smell of the farm intolerable enough to try to get him cited for health violations.

"Used to be people stopped their cars to let us across," the old man said. "I don't give a damn. I been meaning to cut the wire for years now. Even before that dumb place was finished."

He kept kicking in the dirt. "They made a promise, and—" He stopped, and picked something up. A marble.

"And?" Longley said.

His father didn't speak, and Longley knew what it was. It was his other children. The marble belonged to one of his other children, gone now for a quarter of a century. Longley had grown up finding evidence of their existence—toy soldiers, shards of little teacups, obscure toys made of blackened tin, and in the cellar of the house there was always that lingering smell. When he saw the marble his father held he also saw the hairless scarred backs of his fingers. It could only be that. Longley wouldn't speak now. He wouldn't dare intrude—this was a rare moment of what he thought had to be a monumental private grief, so great that all those years couldn't let the old man ever show it. So strangely intense was the set of his face that he could have been a botanist studying a slide.

Longley said, "I'll go back up," and left him there.

He reported the incident of the marble to Noreen, who said, "The poor man. He's got nothing now, what with—"

"Oh Jesus," Longley said, "don't do that to me." He shrugged at the look she gave him and said, "Besides, he's tough as nails." He knew she didn't believe that. Maybe physically, but not otherwise. Even though he looked young for his age despite the scruffy, weatherbeaten look, the death of his wife hadn't done anything to him as far as Noreen was concerned. He never changed, in fact seemed so peculiarly stable that she believed something must be wrong. Someone who acted so sane must be crazy. Longley was tempted to agree with her. When he had told the old man that he wouldn't be coming back to stay, he simply raised his eyebrows and went to the kitchen to get another beer. Then Longley figured that after all it was no problem, and Noreen told him that he had failed to see the obvious.

"But I know what your trouble is," she said. "It's the other kids, right?"

"I don't know. Maybe it's just this place."

"Did you know them?"

"No. Too young."

"In the photographs they look just like you."

Longley went and got a beer.

"It's ten in the morning," she said.

"Nothin' else to do," he said. He looked out the window. The old man was not at the tube any more. "The kids grew up in my mind," he said. "When I was ten or fifteen, I saw them as grown-up versions of the pictures. Older brother and sister."

"The trouble is that they would've stayed, right?"

He sighed. "Probly would. No way of knowin'."

"There's your country drawl again."

"That's a sure sign that it's time to leave."

In the evenings after the old man and his four-hour-a-day hired hand, a kid from the town, did the milking, Longley and Noreen and his father sat on the porch and drank beer or wine and watched the light fade. The porch faced the two-lane highway and pasture and woodland to the south, so they could sit without seeing the shopping center, which would be obscured by the copper glare of the sun sinking into the trees. You could still hear car engines and if the wind was right, music, or the faint hissing sound of the supermarket's automatic doors. The old man always sat in a kind of gloomy corner of the porch, so that he would become a black silhouette by sundown.

This night Longley realized that the tone of the conversation would be different. It became apparent that Noreen was engaged in a kind of gentle, embarrassing cross-examination of the old man's many miseries, as if the last blow of knowing his son was deserting the place needed some helpful verbal contribution from her. And Longley thought, sure, that's how it is—modern people were always eager to get as familiar as possible.

"Why did you build the house in the same place?" she asked.

"C'mon," Longley said, laughing. "What kind of question is that?"

The old man stared at them, then said, "Well, why not? The well's right under us. Foundation's good too."

"No," she said, "I mean in view of the—the fire?"

He drank a half a can of beer and shrugged. "I d'know. Just did it I guess."

"Noreen's just being nosy," Longley said.

Verbal intimacy of this kind made him squirm with embarrassment. She was asking questions he would never dare ask. When the old man got up to get himself another beer, Longley said, "What the hell's going on? Why all this?"

"Don't you realize what a sort of mystery he is?" she asked. "His wife died a few months ago. Doesn't business as usual seem odd to you?"

"Well, he's always like that. He just trucks along. You know, unlike the city types—"

"Like me I suppose."

"—who like to get under the surface of things." He had heard many long analytical speeches from Noreen about her mother and sister and her own problems. He always felt secretly kind of superior to all that, where his own past was concerned. "Nah," he said. "I'm not tryin' to insult you or anything. I'm just sayin' that we aren't the type."

"So you keep stuff in like he does, then."

His father came back to the porch and sat down. "So," he said, "it's business administration or whatever you told me? Big money?"

"I hope so," Longley said.

"What about this place?" Noreen said. "I mean, since we aren't going to—you know."

The old man shrugged, popped the beercan tab and said, "There's a will. She had it done."

"You mean your wife?" Noreen asked.

"Yeah. She was always one for papers and stuff. She said you had to avoid something."

"Probate," Longley said.

"Yeah, probate."

The conversation went on. For Longley, the strange pressure of this all too honest exchange meant too much wine, and inside of an hour his head was pulsing with a dull ache, like heavy, somnolent electricity. Noreen kept up with her bright-faced questioning, at times so obviously trying to be the concerned daughter-in-law that Longley sighed loudly and slapped his forehead, making her briefly glare at him. The black silhouette in the corner, from time to time dully illuminated by the orange tip of the cigarette he drew on, went on talking in the same gravelly monotone. Longley realized that Noreen's questioning indicated more than sympathy for the old man's hidden wretchedness—she seemed to act as if she were more interested in this place and this life than she had led him to believe. "And what's that funny thing with the iron wheels down by the road?"

"It's a side-rake," the old man said, and then went on to explain how it worked.

"C'mon," Longley finally said, "it's nearly bedtime. Let's leave this alone." There was a silence, and Longley could hear faint music.

"It's okay," the old man said. "I ain't talked this much in a long time. No harm. 'Fact after your mother died I hardly talked for a month, 'cept for on the phone with those idiots from the town."

The conversation took a brief, awkward nosedive after that, until Noreen got it back to its original velocity. Then it became too much for him when she began to tread on sacred ground. They looked just like Phil in the pictures. How old were they? Only three and five? That's terrible. It must have been terrible.

And the scars on your fingers. How did they get there? Longley knew, generally, but was quickly stunned by the objective clarity of his father's explanation—he had seen the fire from a distance, in fact just to the left of that goddamned supermarket, over past the pond. He had seen heat boiling the air above the house, dropped the chainsaw, and run. When he got there the house was fully involved. "Involved," he said. "That's a funny word for it. Involved." He climbed the maple tree out front and went out on a branch, then made it to the windowsill of their bedroom. The room was fully involved, and the two children were pinned in a corner screaming and holding onto each other. The fire going up the wall burned his fingers until he lost his grip and fell.

There was a silence, during which Longley visualized the scene. Then his father leaned forward and cleared his throat. "They danced," he said softly.

"What?" Longley said.

"They danced. When the fire got to them, just before I fell—" He took a deep breath and blew it out. "Caroline put her arms around Chuck, and then they started spinning, sort of stamping their feet like they was dancing. Their hair was on fire. Then I fell."

Again, in the silence, Longley could hear the music and the hissing of the supermarket doors. Noreen stared at the silhouette with the little orange point of light against it. Her mouth was half open, and she said nothing.

"It was a long time ago," the old man said. Longley had never heard this before, and tried to imagine it, because it was worse than any of the pictures he had imagined. They danced.

"It was damn lucky Phil was out with his mother," he went on. "She could see the smoke all the way from town."

"Did they find out what caused it?" Noreen asked.

"Chimney fire," he said.

It seemed there was nothing left to say now. The old man rose from his chair, collected up his beer cans, and said, "I gotta go to bed. Tomorrow they either clear the tube or I cut the wire."

"Hey," Longley said, glad that the subject was a matter of the present, "wake me up, okay? We'll do the tube. Leave the wire alone. Those people are mad enough at you already."

"Sure," the old man said, "because cows shit. Excuse me." He looked at Noreen. "A barnyard is a barnyard, and if they don't like it, then they can put the shopping center someplace else."

"Gotcha," Longley said, "but I'll help you clean the tube anyway."

After he left they sat in silence, and Longley imagined that Noreen, too, was going over in her mind what it must have been like to watch your children die like that. Then she whispered, "My God, they danced."

Later, when he sat down on the edge of the bed and wound the old clock, he considered what hour to set it for, and decided on seven, after the milking would be done. When he got under the covers she rolled to him, sending her breath against his neck, and he responded immediately—she was right. It was a like a magnetism that negated the horror of what they had been told, and the best way to escape back into the present.

But Longley slept badly, his imagination invaded by dream images spun off his father's story. And when he was awake, he couldn't get that picture out of his mind, of children dancing, their hair on fire. His brother and sister. He had never heard his father get that precise about it. Noreen's questioning brought it out of him in a matter of a couple of hours, as if Longley, having lived with him for so long, had failed to learn anything about him simply because he had neglected to ask. What he knew were surfaces, embarrassing habits, silly exploits, gruffness. But then he thought, so what? People always seemed obsessed by what was under the surface, and he disliked the assumption that digging at people's secrets was good for them. It seemed almost like a compromise of their individuality. We do what we do and that's that. In a hundred years none of this will make any difference anyway.

And before he finally slept he thought, I will not get worked up over this. Tomorrow it's the business of the present, to head off another embarrassment.

He got up before seven in the morning and found Noreen sitting at the kitchen table drinking coffee. "Mornin', hot stuff," he said.

She giggled, but had a peculiar look on her face.

"...'s'matter?" he asked.

She shook her head. "This is gruesome—I was going to have a cookout tonight."

Longley laughed. "No no, don't worry about it," he said.

"I'm serious," she said. "It's like a sick joke."

"He'll never make the connection."

"I will."

"Nah, don't worry about it. Where is he?"

"He's down at the tube with that kid and the cows. God, I couldn't think of anything but those kids."

Longley stepped to the window and looked. He could see his father gesturing to the kid and pointing across the highway. "Oh Jesus, he's gonna do it. What day is it?"

"Saturday."

"There'll be dozens of people there in no time." Noreen came to the window, and then laughed.

"Well, there's something tangible for you, If you're too full of history," she said.

He snorted softly. "Yeah, good point," he said. "Look, I'm goin' down there. That place opens at seven today."

"Go ahead. I'll get some better shoes."

Longley ran down the long slope toward the herd of cows. His father smiled when he saw him.

"Hey, give us a hand here, buck. We're goin' across."

Out of breath, Longley said, "Wait," and waved his hands quickly. "Wait, let's—think this over."

The hired hand's face was a mask of anxious doubt, and Longley said, "Your time's up today, right?"

"It is," the kid said. "I mean it really is."

"Go on along then," Longley said. "It's okay."

"I'm payin' him, you know," the old man said. But the kid was already gone.

"Let's cut this out," Longley said. He looked across the bony backs of the cows. Even the docile old bull was with them. His father was at the fence, cutters in hand, his face crossed with an uncharacteristic look of excitement.

"Go look in the vat," he said. "Little trickle of water. Take all day to water them. This is the only way."

"How do you expect to keep them from goin' all over?"

"Montrose here goes where I tell him. The rest follow."

"Montrose is senile," Longley said. "He has bovine Alzheimer's Disease. He goes where he feels like." He looked around and saw Noreen coming down the slope. Then he heard the first twangy clip sound amid snufflings and scraping of hooves. He could see the rusted wire snaking slowly on the ground. When he heard the second clip, and the high pitched twang, he pulled into himself and began to calculate strategy—stop the traffic, keep them over to the left of the parking lot, get the other fence cut before they bunch along it. There was no more reason to talk. If the old man wanted to do this, then he would do it, and Longley would consider himself a casual observer. Whatever disasters occurred would be none of his business.

Noreen positioned herself on the two-lane highway to stop traffic, at first smiling at Longley and mimicking a football player, jumping around in a defensive crouch. The traffic appeared of course just as Longley heard the clacking of the cows' hooves on the macadam. His father drove Montrose with a broom handle, and the cows rumped along slowly behind him, their bags swaying. It would work, after all. Longley smiled at the four cars waiting, two of them with kids leaning out of the windows to watch. He adopted a jovial, businesslike air—sure folks, we do this all the time, no problem.

But Longley believed that what could go wrong would go wrong, and nodded ruefully to himself when he saw the two men come out the hissing doors of the supermarket, one wearing a red blazer, the other a red apron. He thought the story about bulls and red was baloney, at least as far as dimwitted Holsteins were concerned. No, it was not the color that worried him—it was the expression on the first man's face—a mixture of surprise and a kind of bulldog, confrontational directness. Longley figured he'd better act as spokesman. The problem was that he was bringing up the rear, gently slapping cows' rumps, and the two men were closer to his father, who paid no attention to them. A car horn honked, spooking the cows closest to Noreen. They jostled toward the center of the herd, making one highboned cow rise up and struggle forward, for a few steps riding the back of the cow in front of her.

People came out of the little stores next to the super-market and watched. Then the closeness of the two men began to divide the herd. "Hold on!" Longley yelled. "Stay back!"

But the manager was not interested in waiting. He marched along the fence bordering the parking lot toward Longley's father.

"Cut the fence!" Longley yelled. He heard the manager in the red blazer ask his father something like, "Who authorized you to do this?" and Mr. Longley waved him away. He said, "Back off now. B'with you in a minute."

Longley decided to go to the front of the herd. He ran around the cows toward the manager. "Listen," he said, "if you'd just stand back—"

"And who might I ask are you?" the manager asked. His forehead glistened with a sheen of sweat.

"Once he cuts the fence everything'll be okay."

"When the smell comes from up there it's bad enough," the man said, "but there'll be hell to pay for this."

Longley bristled with a sudden defensive anger. "Oh yeah? Who says?" And he thought, my God, what a stupid thing to say. And almost as if to prove the validity of the manager's point, one of the cows near him raised her tail, and during the sustained splatting sound, the manager appeared to simply listen studiously. Longley felt the heat of embarrassment rise into his face. When the cow was finished, the manager said, "Precisely," and moved toward Longley's father, who had cut two of the four wires on the fence.

"Hey, back off!" he snapped. "You'll spook the cows!"

Longley flushed with shame, and looked toward Noreen, who was talking with one of the people in the first car, which began to edge slowly around the space behind the herd.

Then everything went wrong at once. A semi coming from the other direction stopped at the herd, but the hissing of its brakes along with a loud screech sent a third of the cows behind Longley straight for the supermarket doorway. That drew the cows next to Longley in the direction of the others, and suddenly Montrose slid past the manager, who was up against the wall with his arms raised as if he were standing chest deep in water, his face ashen.

"Stop 'em over there!" Longley's father yelled, and Longley headed for the doors.

He didn't make it. As the cows filed inside, he tried to bull his way between them but ended up sandwiched by their huge, soft bellies, unable to keep any firm contact with the ground under him. He was carried inside by two cows. The sudden blast of cool air and the crazy multitude of different colors reduced his mind to a strange dream state. He was vaguely aware of a few customers and checkout girls and clerks moving to one side of the store, some laughing, some stumbling back with their mouths open.

Then he was brushed in the ribs by a horn, and gave up and stepped to one side. He was overcome with a sensation of bemused distance, watching the cows, who bunched at a narrow opening to the interior of the store. One cow slipped on the gleaming tile floor so that her back legs slid outward in a painful-looking split. As she struggled to regain her footing, he said, "Easy now, girl, that's it—make believe it's ice."

He heard the rapid voice of the manager behind him somewhere, along with the apologetic, I-told-you-so drawl of his father. Noreen too. Then someone was at his side, a young blond-haired grocery clerk. "It appears we have a little, ah, problem here," Longley said.

The clerk giggled, amazed. "Whoops, boss comin'," he whispered, and vanished.

Longley realized that he'd been letting the cows pass without stopping them. "Thanks a bunch," the manager said from the doorway. Longley shrugged, and the manager passed by him and went for the phone. Police, of course.

Longley went further into the store area, aware that his father and Noreen were following.

Montrose, senile or not, still had a good nose. He had made his way down a lane of juices, coffee and tea, various displays of nuts, then past powdered milk, cereals, and a little display of Oriental foods right to the vegetable section. By the time Longley was able to make his way there, a third of the cows were lined up at the bins, watched from close up by two young store workers. They slapped each other's hands and celebrated like victorious athletes, frequently whispering and peeking around the shelves, probably looking for the manager.

And the store's few shoppers found the spectacle worth watching. One woman even drew out a little camera from her purse and began taking flash pictures.

"Well for chrissakes," his father said from behind him.

"I think it would be wise to leave them alone," Longley said.

After some unimportant jostling, the cows had managed to position themselves in a line facing the bins. They chewed blissfully on cabbage, corn, lettuce, particularly the romaine and leaf lettuces. "Look there," Longley said to Noreen. "What is she eating?"

"Watercress, I think," she said, her voice cracked with awe.

"Make sure they don't eat the apples," Longley said.

"No," his father said, "they don't see them yet." The apples were in separate bins behind the cows.

Suddenly the store manager was face to face with Longley's father, who leaned back with wide-eyed surprise. The manager poked his index finger toward the old man's nose and said, "I want them out now! Do you hear me? I want them out now!"

He said other things, which Longley didn't hear, because he was mesmerized with anger at the man, particularly by the bright red of his jacket. He found himself turning the man around and then gathering the red lapels in his fists, and then backing the man up against the nearest cow.

"You know what we're doin'?" Longley asked.

The man shook his head quickly.

Longley crushed the lapels with his fists. "We're waiting for the police, right?" The man nodded. "So you're going to keep your mouth closed, okay?" The man stared at him. "Right?" Longley said. "Am I right?" The man nodded quickly, and Longley let him go. "Good," he said.

When he turned around, Noreen and his father were staring at him, and then at each other. "Sorry," Longley said. "I don't like him is all."

During the five minutes it took for the police to get to the store, Longley and his father chatted with a kind of shrugging amiability with clerks and patrons, who had settled into watching the feast with the studiousness of people seeing an interesting display at a zoo.

Once, with a tentative impulse to experiment, Longley's father tried to move the five cows closest to the doors away from the vegetables, but they did what cows do when you try that—although they chewed a little faster, with a mild, dewey-eyed alarm, they ignored the urging and leaned against him, easily offsetting the pressure of his hands.

Longley began to worry about bloat, and asked his father about it. "No," he said. "There ain't enough. They'll finish and look for more. I don't know about some of this stuff though. Hey—" and he gestured to a clerk. "What's that stuff over there?"

"Uh, okra?"

Longley watched the cows chew up the funny, podlike vegetables.

"And that?" Mr. Longley asked, pointing.

"Ginger root," he said. "I don't think they like it."

They didn't. The two cows closest to it worked on other obscure vegetables on either side. Two other clerks who had the good sense to predict what would be next began covering the fruits in separate bins with huge, oily tarpaulins. "Good idea," Mr. Longley called to them. "Besides, I don't want them eating oranges and plums and stuff like that."

The manager appeared at the other end of the line of cows, now settled into a hopeless acceptance of the situation. He looked carefully down the bins, nodding slowly as if to say, yes, yes, that too, yes, ninety-eight cents a pound, one twenty-nine a pound.

Longley was able to maintain his attitude of business-like joviality through the newspaper interview. He kept his composure and speculated on how to pay for all the food—"Well, I suppose an average per pound value, and of course a cleaning fee—" Then, the police interview, during which the two town cops had some trouble con-trolling sudden bursts of laughter.

Once the vegetables were gone, it was surprisingly easy to herd the cows out the door, through the fence and to the pond. Two of the younger clerks helped, all the time yelling, "Head 'em up, move 'em out," and "Git the sodbusters out of the way!" and the manager looked on with an acid stare. None of the cows protested—if anything they seemed mesmerized by the fading awareness of what they had just tasted. As for damage, there was little. Cows may appear clumsy but are not. Left alone, they got about their business with something approaching delicacy. There were only crushed cereal boxes and one overturned bookrack loaded with romance novels, which, according to one sympathetic customer, was knocked over only because a clerk had scared the pretty little Jersey with those big, liquid eyes. She went off course and hooked her horn in the wire rack. It was not her fault.

Longley was surprised to discover that it was only 8:30 in the morning. As the three of them walked back up the hill, his father way out in front because he was going to call the road department again, Longley worked in his mind on an appropriate attitude—he didn't really feel any particular anger toward his father, nor did he feel embarrassed. In fact if he felt anything, it was a kind of sophomoric pleasure at having shut the pompous manager up.

"I'll bet that never happened before," Noreen said.

"There you have an example of what can happen when my father gets an idea," he said. "Wait'll you see the bill."

In the house once again, he had the sudden sensation that the incident hadn't happened. It was as if an event even as garish as this couldn't compete with the weight of the past. And as tough as his father was, he couldn't escape it either. His story of the children dancing with their hair on fire proved that.

Longley went through the day by himself. His father worked out somewhere on fences, and Noreen went into town to shop. During his aimless pacing around the house, he passed the open door leading to the attic stairway, and went up. There was no reason to go because he knew what was up there, but he went anyway.

The dusty little half circle of a window at one end of the attic threw a pale light over boxes, a few old pieces of furniture and some trunks, stuff that had been stored at the back of the woodshed of the old house. Useless even a quarter of a century ago, it was all the town fire department could save. He wandered down the cleared center lane on the squeaking tongue-and-groove flooring, and saw way off in the distance through the window his father pushing a locust fencepost up straight and propping it in place with a piece of two-by-four.

Longley turned to leave, then stopped. Down at his feet were boxes that he knew contained some of the things that had belonged to the other kids. He opened the one closest. Inside were a few picture books and a rolled up sheaf of drawing paper, which he picked up and opened. The paper was dry, almost brittle, so he bent it open to peer in at the curved surface of a crayon drawing of a stick-man, below which were scrawled the angular letters forming a name. Caroline L. He put the pictures back in the box. He was held in a strange, ticklish half-memory, visualizing her. Suddenly vaguely uneasy, he thought he should leave. But that strange sensation, almost like a swoon where he felt half numb, stayed with him, and then gradually, like something slowly coming into focus in his awareness, he felt their presence in the shadows, even thought he heard a kind of whispering. He stood very still.

The sensation of fear he thought he felt began to change, so that the presence of the two dead children, like a peculiar, enveloping vapor, was no threat—it seemed only to be the shadows of a sad fact, and standing there, he felt himself absorb whatever populated the space he stood in. He looked around, then heard the screen door downstairs slap shut.

His father was sitting in the kitchen waiting for the coffee to heat up. Longley went to the sink and washed the black dust off his hands.

"...'cha been doin'?" his father asked.

"Nothin', just pokin' in the attic."

His father poured his coffee. "I don't like to go up there," he said. Longley looked at him questioningly, and he said, "It's funny—after we built this place your mother used to go up there. Couple times I even heard her talkin'." He shook his head, looking down at the table. "Never told anybody that." He chuckled, seeming to remember it. "Then, later I started thinkin' of them as still around too, up where their stuff is. Each year I'd see them as a little bigger—you know, older even though they was dead." He drank his coffee in one long gulp.

Longley stared at the middle distance between himself and his father. The old man then slapped his knees and stood up. "I just don't like goin' up there," he said, heading for the door.


The light breeze prevented the sound of the supermarket doors from reaching the porch. Longley and Noreen sat watching the old man start the fire with newspapers in the stone pit out in the yard. The cows, now already milked and out in the pasture up the hill from the house, had been easily herded back through the tube under the highway. The town maintenance crew did the job at three o'clock in the afternoon. Mr. Longley had said, just after the job was done, "See? That's all it takes—a little stampede in a supermarket and bingo, the job's done."

It was nearly dusk, and they watched the dark form illuminated by the flames, appearing and disappearing in the smoke.

"I shouldn't have worried about the cookout," Noreen said. "You do what you do."

"I guess," Longley said. "But he's not really as far from it as I thought. He does think about it."

"Who wouldn't?"

Longley drank some of his beer. "The chicken and stuff ready?"

"Yeah, all set." She leaned forward and put her elbows on her knees. "He apologized to me for this morning."

"What'd he say?"

"Just 'look, I'm sorry for putting you in that situation.' You know what I said? I told him it was beautiful."

"That's 'cause it was."

"And he said you sure surprised him by grabbing that manager. How's it feel to have an enemy?"

"Okay. Kind of normal, as a matter of fact."

She looked out at the old man. "Listen," she said, "I've been thinking."

"So have I."

"It doesn't necessarily mean anything, but really, just until the calf is born, okay?"

"Okay," he said. Then he laughed. "Hey, should we try going to the supermarket?"

"Why not?" she said. "It's a free country."

Longley thought of the manager, and any trace of shame he might have felt was gone. He was left only with the sensation of surprise that he had done it, along with a recognition that seemed alien to him but still agreeable, that he would do it again.

# The Outsider

Magnified inside the bright, watery circle of the rifle scope, she seemed to Steven Dials almost close enough to call to. She wore a faded plaid shirt with the sleeves cut off and denim shorts, and she kicked the horse to a gallop along the hayfield road, close to the wooded knoll where he sat. He could see through the cross hairs the frothy sweat of the horse around the bridle and the fine halo of the girl's blonde hair. He whispered, "Jeanette Anderson," slowly swinging the rifle as she passed below him. Then, afraid that the glass of the scope might bounce the sun and give him away, he lowered the rifle and carefully faded back into the woods.

He had taken the rifle from a summer house a mile up the dirt road he lived on. The house belonged to some older city people who used it only in late August, and it had been easy to break into. It was small, but inside had a sort of plush quality, and he had found the bolt action .22 in a closet. The scope was a new six-power, oily and black. He also found two boxes of long rifle hollow point cartridges. At first he had spent two weeks shooting woodchucks and birds, far enough away from the house that no one would know, until he used up all but ten of the cartridges. It was on one of his walks into the woods that he had found Jeanette Anderson's place on another dirt road. What held him at first was the clean, organized, well-painted look of their farm, as if it came straight from *Farm Journal* or *Successful Farming*. He had lived here only six months. He didn't know Jeanette Anderson, but he did remember that she rode the school bus and was picked up before he and his cousins were.

After he hunted or watched for Jeanette Anderson, he would check the sun and then have to hurry through the woods to get back before his uncle came home around four o'clock, time to get the cows. The only problem was to make sure no one saw the rifle. The kids would tell, his aunt might know where it came from, and in any case they knew he owned no rifle.

But today he got back in plenty of time. His legs a little shaky, he hid the rifle on a high shelf behind the bull's pen in a cobwebbed depression behind a beam. Sometimes when he climbed up to put it away, he would aim the rifle at the house through a small window to see who was there—his aunt might appear, sweeping past the cross hairs, inside the kitchen window, or he would see one of the kids by the outhouse.

He knew they all thought something was a little strange about him. By early summer, after he had been there five months, he had begun sleeping in the barn. One of the boys was a bedwetter and he didn't like the smell, all crowded in the room with them. There were no beds in the boys' room, and the four of them slept on discarded clothing on the floor. The two girls slept on bunks in a walk-in closet off the parents' room. Nobody seemed to care about his sleeping in the barn except his aunt, who thought it was improper. But he got away with it, and that was a relief, because he preferred being alone in the warm, dusty manger, breathing air that was almost sweet with the smells of hay and grain and fermented cows' breath.

He didn't fit in, but he was part of this family, which meant eating what they ate and taking nearly the same beatings that the other kids did. Once he dropped a pail of milk in the cellar drive, and his uncle whacked him on the side of the head so hard that he saw stars. He found himself blinking at the milk running into and becoming pea-green in the soft summer manure in the gutter. "You gonna keep your head about you?" his uncle asked.

"Yes," he said.

"You got to—you got to keep your head."

Steven's cousin Robert, older by a month, had said later, in a conspiratorial whisper, "Welcome to the goddam club," and then added, "He always does that. You gotta watch out."

Now, after hiding the rifle, he sat in the manger near his blanket and pillow, waiting for the truck. When he heard the familiar sound of pebbles plinking the insides of fenders out in the driveway, he felt a swoon of dread. It was four o'clock. He rose and went out the back to get the cows.

There was nothing he could do about where he lived or how he lived. He hated the school and had signed his quitting papers in June, which his uncle figured was a good idea because it meant another hand around while he was out working for the county road. So he was another hand. In school there was nothing he could do really except draw, but that meant nothing. In the spring, just after he had moved in with his uncle's family, he did a picture of a horse and rider in the manner of Frederick Remington, and the teacher had been impressed enough to hang it on the wall. After a day it was crudely revised by someone using a red pen, and he ripped if off the wall and threw it away, his face flushed with shame. He looked forward to an end to the embarrassment of going to school. From his old house he had gone smelling like gasoline and pinesap and stovewood smoke, and now it was manure and turned milk, and he couldn't shake the smell by getting on the bus.

Most of growing up for him had come down to helping his father cut pulpwood, since he was six or seven. All his jeans had holes above the right knee, from the way you had to pick the four-foot chunks up, seesawing them in order to struggle them up onto truck beds. It was one of those days in early spring when he had skipped school, his other school, that his father had tried to drag a log up a hill and flipped the tractor back over on himself. Steven had run to him, watching the huge, cleated wheels still spinning, and got down on his knees to ask his father if he was all right. His head was mashed partway into the cold mud and twisted sideways too far, and the tractor had crushed his folded body. His face was swollen, his tongue seemed to crowd his half-open mouth, and all he could do was blink once before he died.

It seemed no time at all before he ended up here, a house very much like his own, surrounded by broken-down farm equipment, dirt paths where people walked, snaking through weeds and burdock bushes, soggy cardboard and woodchips in the dirt driveway, and inside the kitchen, where everyone sat, linoleum with its pattern worn off where you walked, and a table with a plastic cloth topped with sticky rings from milk glasses and coffee cups.

Like his father, who barely subsisted on pulpwood, his uncle was as mean as he was because he barely made it shipping milk. It took him only a month to realize that all he had to do was wait it out two years and join the service, as his brother had done. And waiting, watching the days, was a kind of subtle flexing of his whole body, almost like holding your breath for two years.

On his free time in the summer he sneaked into the woods with the stolen rifle, while the others sat and watched TV or did whatever they did. Once a week he would wear his bathing trunks under his clothes and go down to Ryder's Bridge and the creek, to take a bath, he supposed, although he used no soap. During those times when he could hear voices of swimmers through the woods, he would put it off. When he heard nothing, he would hide the rifle and go down to swim.

On one of those trips in late July he could hear the usual yelling and splashing from a distance, but decided to hide the gun and go to the bridge anyway.

It turned out that the yelling came from one person, Jeanette Anderson, and when he recognized her he felt a sudden wave of shame. Of course, her house was less than a mile up the road. He was about to leave when he saw her climb up the bank and then walk up the rusty steel incline of the bridge frame. She wore a red two-piece bathing suit, and he could see the trail of water drips and footprints and handprints she left in the rust as she climbed. It seemed insanely dangerous to him because she was probably twenty-five feet above the water and fifteen feet above the broken macadam of the road. Then she began to yell: "I claim all lands I can see as belonging to me and me alone, in the sovereign kingdom of—"

She saw him. He froze where he was, wondering what to do. She had covered her mouth with her hand

and suddenly seemed unsure of her balance. Then she continued shouting: "Who goes there? You, stranger! I recognize you from the bus! Come down here and state your infernal business!" Then she jumped, arms out, hair flying above her head, and entered the water in a half cannonball. She surfaced laughing.

He made his way through the brush to the bank of the creek, trying to think of something to say. He looked around.

"You're the one who lives with the Dials family," she said.

"Yeah."

She was treading water in the deep part, her pale limbs surreal and misshapen through the water. Then she swam to the bank and went for her towel.

"Hey," she said, "on the bridge there. That's just stupid playing. Don't tell."

"Okay."

"So how's it over to the Dials' place?"

"Fine. Okay."

"Well," she said, "if you're gonna swim, go ahead."

While she dried herself, her back turned to him, he quickly got out of his jeans and shirt and boots and stuffed them under a bush. He went into the water disregarding the shocking cold. The breeze blew from her past his clothing, so he figured she wouldn't smell them. He moved around in the water vigorously to keep warm, and in a little while saw her climbing the bridge tower again. Then, from the top, she called, "Hey wait, watch. Back away." He moved toward the shallow water. "You down there! Peasant! Commoner!" She struck a stance of pompous oratory, swinging her arms as if addressing a huge crowd. "I have spent years purifying this property of usurpers! You have contaminated water which hitherto could have been bottled.  I find this—" and then she jumped, and in midair yelled, "marginally—" went in, and surfaced, shouting, "tolerable!"  He looked at her, shaking his head. "Stupid, huh?" she said.  "It's because I had to read Shakespeare last year."

She went off the bridge yelling three more times, until she was exhausted and hoarse and he was so cold that he had to get out.  He stood on the bank shivering, with his arms wrapped around himself, and waited to be dry enough to put his clothes back on.  When she had dried herself, she said, "What, no towel?" and threw hers to him.  He dried himself quickly and threw it back.  In what seemed like no time at all, she had run up on the bank with her towel and was off on a beat-up old bicycle.

He sat in the sun, wondering about the peculiar, sort of automatic familiarity of the towel.  He wondered why nobody had ever been that—and he wondered what the right word was.  Familiar.  Nobody had ever been that familiar with him before.  Then he saw his shadow on the ground and mentally superimposed on it a picture of the drive between the barn mangers and bolted in a muttering panic for his clothes.

He was too late.  Through the scope he could see Hal and Billy, the two younger boys, chasing a cow in the driveway near his uncle's truck, and his uncle and Robert hunched at the barnyard fence.  He knew what was wrong. Bunched at the barn door, some of the cows were always pushed up against a rickety section of wooden fence and had probably gone through.  It was precisely what his uncle had warned him against.  He had to hide the rifle in the woods, hundreds of yards from the house.  And then he ran, feeling the odd sensation of being overcome with haste to get to his punishment.

But it was not as bad as he expected. With a hammer in one hand, his uncle reached out, blew a nail from his mouth, and took the upper part of Steven's shirt and crushed it in his other hand. Then he backed him up against the barn wall and pushed his fist into his throat. Robert stood behind watching, his face twisted with an expression of vicarious pain.

"I can't use a worthless jerk around here," his uncle said. "Understand?" His uncle twisted his fist into his throat. "Don't be a worthless jerk. Okay?"

Steven felt a strange rush in his head, a flash of secret rebellion that apparently did something to his expression, because Robert was now shaking his head quickly and mouthing the word, no.

"Understand?" his uncle said. Now Robert was waving his hands at him. Finally Steven was let go, and his uncle went back to repairing the fence. Steven got ready to say something—who the hell said I was supposed to do this in the first place?—but Robert's pantomiming kept him silent.

When his uncle left, he said, "He says things twice, you notice that?"

Robert laughed. "What you don't want is when he says things four times. Man, I thought you were gonna spit in his face."

"Nah," Steven said. "So what do you do, anyway?"

"Keep your mouth shut and be careful," Robert said. "Me? I'm outta here as soon's I can go. You know half of why I play football and basketball in school?" He glanced at the house. "It's the school lunches, the time off, and the showers. I'm not that good in sports, but I'm not that bad either. Mostly it's the showers."

"Can't your parents—I mean—"

"When you got no money you can't do much. That's about it."

On his walks through the woods, he now wore his trunks every time, but did not see Jeanette Anderson down at the bridge for three days. Through the cross hairs of the scope there were only the horseflies hovering over the water. He no longer went to the knoll above her house because it now seemed improper, because he knew her.

On the fourth day she was there again, and when he saw her, he quickly lowered the rifle, hid it, and went down to the creek. And she talked with that same strange familiarity that had mystified him before. Once, when she came out of the water to dry off and warm up, she said, "My Dad said your father was killed in an accident." He nodded. "Were you there?"

He flushed and said, "N—no. I mean, yes, yes I was."

"Oh," she said. "Well, you don't hafta— I guess I shouldn't've asked."

"No. It's okay." But he didn't know what to say beyond that. "You—you got a nice lookin' farm."

She looked at the water, then around at the trees. Then she said, "What's it like living with the Dials family? I mean, I'm not nosy—I mean that your cousin's sorta semi girlfriend told me some, well, some sorta horror stories."

He shrugged. "It's okay. My uncle's got lots to worry about."

"Well," she said, "if you don't wanna say, forget it—but their—situation's kind of, uh, known here, I guess."

"It's not bad," he said. Then he went on to tell her that he planned to wait it out two years and go into the service, that he'd already quit school, and that the situation, as she called it, didn't really make any difference to him.

"You shouldn't quit school," she said. "I thought you were going into art school or something. So they said anyway."

He flushed again and made a face. "Art don't mean nothin'," he said. "Who's 'they'?"

"Teachers. My mother works at the library sometimes."

He looked at the shadow on the ground. "It's after three," he said. "I gotta go." He got up and went over to the bush where his clothes were and decided to carry them into the woods before putting them back on. "See ya," he said and left her there.

After he got dressed he walked back through the woods with the gun cradled in his elbow, grimacing to himself because there was something almost horrible about a personal conversation. He had never had one of these before, and the sensation was awful—it created a kind of shaky feeling, and it was so alien to him that he wondered if he could stand to do it again.

That same day, still distracted by the strange feeling about the conversation, he drove the tractor and a spreader load of manure across the driveway toward a stubbled hayfield and grazed too close to his uncle's truck. The back wheel of the old spreader hooked the rear bumper and pulled it partway off. Right away everyone, even the two girls, stood at the back door of the house, and his uncle came up, pulled him off the tractor, and stung him on the side of the head with an open handed blow. "Look at that," he said. "Look at that. A driveway this big, and will you look!" Steven was dizzy and couldn't open his left eye, and he gazed at the others and saw them as a bright, flat, two-dimensional picture, like a cartoon. He giggled. His uncle pushed him away and he sat down so that all the air exploded from his lungs. When he felt that he had come somewhat to his senses, he saw Robert waving at him to keep quiet. He stood up and tried to speak. "You—I'm—" Then he turned and went into the barn. His temple throbbed and his eye ran, but he could open it a little.

He walked down the drive, vaguely aware that it was time to get the cows. He went into the bull's pen, climbed up on the slats and pulled the rifle out of the cobwebbed depression. Then he turned, flicked the safety off, and aimed it out the window. His uncle was kneeling by the truck in profile, and he placed the cross hairs against his face. He felt a strange, airy lightness, as if he had no substance. Inside the bright circle he saw his uncle's mouth move—his face was so big that it filled the scope, and he could see the cracks in his skin, the black and gray stubble of his cheek, the large red ear, and the oily fabric of his hat. His uncle blinked. Steven became dizzy, and the watery circle swept down his uncle's shirt. When he realized what he was doing, he threw the rifle back behind the beam and scrambled down from the window, shaking so badly that he could barely stand up. He went and sat down near where he slept and put his aching face down in his hands. He was fully awake now and knew that he had come within a half a second of pulling the trigger.

The next day, when he made it to the woods, he turned and went in the opposite direction from his usual walks—and he ran rather than walked, the gun in his right hand. He stopped once, about halfway, and put his hand to his throbbing head. Once he got his breath he was aware that he was surrounded by chickadees. The friendliest bird in the world. "And I shot them," he said. And then he whispered, "Oh God," and ran the rest of the way to the old people's summer house. He replaced the rifle where he had found it, a little sad that there were so few bullets left and that the stock now had scratches on it. Then he tried to replace the part of the door sill that he had broken and closed the place up again.

He was still overcome with a sensation of haste and ran back into the woods, disregarding the pain that flashed into his head with each step. After a while, when he had managed to slow himself to a fast walk, he realized what it was—if it had not been for Jeanette Anderson, his uncle would now be dead. He didn't know why this was true, but as he climbed the bluff that opened out to the bridge and creek, he knew there was a connection.

She was not there. He sat on the bank, watching the water, and waited for her until his shadow got too long, and then rose to go back and get the cows.

The next day, when he was free, he experienced the same feeling of haste and ran through the woods to get to the bridge, convinced that she would not be there. But she was, and he had to hold himself back from running down the bluff. He walked, thinking, this is stupid, this is ridiculous.

"What happened to your head?" she asked. "It's all bruised."

"Accident," he said. Then he shook his head. "Okay, I got hit."

She didn't say anything. She seemed to be thinking of an appropriate response. Then she said, "Well, you gonna swim?"

He had forgotten his trunks. Stupid. "Nah, not today," he said. Then he sighed and looked at the woods. "Okay. I forgot my trunks." He began to feel embarrassed as the odor of sweat and manure and turned milk rose from his shirt into his face. He backed away from her.

"What's wrong?"

He shook his head and decided to leave. Then he laughed, feeling a sensation of strange recklessness. "My clothes stink," he said. She looked away, apparently a little embarrassed. "They always stink," he said. "All my life. Ain't nothin' to be done about it."

Then he looked at the water, and the feeling of recklessness surged into his chest, and he ran down the bank and dove in with his clothes on. When he surfaced, he said, "I don't care how long it takes—they gotta dry sometime, right?"

"What do you do in the winter?" she asked, laughing.

"Wait till summer."

After that day he knew it was inevitable that August would end and she would be going back to school and he would be left as an extra hand. He did his work, he went through the woods each day, and she was there again swimming, only a few days before school would start. The conversation went on—you can't let him treat you that way, she told him. You're supposed to have rights. And he told her that he was waiting it out and it wasn't really as bad as all that. She showed in her face that she didn't believe him and climbed the bridge. His shadow got too long, and that was that.

But one day he tried to swing one of the hundred-pound cans into the cooler and spilled a gallon of milk out of the top because the cover of the can was on too loosely. This time, instead of looking at his uncle, he put the cover back on and swung the can into the cooler, and then went down to the house, since there was nothing more to do. His uncle caught up with him in the woodshed, grabbed him by the shirt, and rammed him against the wall. "Nice work, jerk," he said, and cuffed him on the bruise from the last time. "That's a jerk's work, boy," he said, and rammed him against the wall again, and then went inside for coffee. Steven could hear his aunt asking what was wrong, and heard his uncle use the word "jerk" again.

He went into the kitchen. They were sitting at the table, his uncle, aunt, and Robert. The kids were watching TV in the other room.

He stood in the doorway and said, "My father beat the crap outta me and that was his right. You got no right."

Robert shook his head quickly, his eyes wide with fright.

His uncle sat, coffee cup in hand, and looked at Steven with an expression of belligerent surprise.

"Who says?" his uncle said.

"We're in the house now," his aunt said. "Let's stop this now."

"I say," Steven said. "You don't know nothin' about me. You hardly even know who I am. I don't know why you push people around—that's your business. But you got no right."

"...'at a fact?" his uncle said. He moved, as if to rise from his chair. Robert began to squirm, shaking his head.

"Yeah, that there is a fact," Steven said. "I'm not your kid. I'm my father's kid, and he's dead." His uncle thought a moment and then seemed to relax. Then he shrugged.

"Well, if you say so," he said, and made a clucking sound with his mouth. "Well, how do you like that?"

"And I'm goin' back to school."

"What for?"

"I don't know. All I know is I'm going back. That's my right too."

"You gonna draw pictures?" his uncle asked mockingly.

"Yeah, that's what I'm gonna do. Pictures." Then he left.

Later, Robert seemed amazed at the kitchen scene. "What did you say that made him click?"

"Beats me," Steven said.

"I can't believe this."

"Well, after all, who says it has to be like sunrise and sunset?"

Robert thought a moment and said, "Yeah, I guess."

Once Steven had committed himself, he had to go through with it, smelly clothes or not. He made one last trip to the bridge and swam clothed, and spent the day feeling them dry. He supposed his aunt would have done them, but he didn't want to ask. And on the morning the bus came, he got on, walked to the back, and sat by the window, past all the people sitting in the rows. Jeanette Anderson was sitting with another girl and looked at him as he passed. When he had settled into his seat, he looked out the window at the brown hay stubble streaming along the roadside, thinking, stupid, absolutely stupid. He already felt embarrassed.

She came to the back, rocking with the movement of the bus, and sat down next to him. "What?" he said.

"Can I sit here?"

"Sure."

She was looking at him, smiling, apparently expecting him to say something. "What made you change your mind?"

He shrugged. "I don't know." Then he said, "Well, maybe you did." She didn't hear him because she was waving at her friend that she would stay where she was. "I said you did. You changed my mind."

Then she leaned across to the window to look out. Her face was less than a foot from his, and he saw it in such minute detail that he was momentarily almost shocked.

"There's our place," she said, and then he felt the bus bump up to the bridge macadam and watched the rusty girders go by. "You wait'll we go there in the winter," she said. "It's a honey of a place to skate."

# The Red House

So maybe now it's down to the woods.

"I shoveled the gutters, washed milk pails." The way he looks now at the table, no wonder men in town call him The Chimp. "I'm goin' to the woods."

A snort. Looks up from an oily dismantled carbure-tor on the plastic tablecloth crisscrossed white and red, his creased, stubbly face blank. Grins. "Honey on your stinger?"

"No, just walkin'." Sort of told him from the edge three times that it's the float lever shaft, that it's bent, or lost, or sheared off, but he won't pick up the clue and so that old tractor won't ever work right. Right there in the *Operator's Manual*. But the last time he had that look, you say that once more and you'll lose some teeth.

Out. The woodshed walls gray melting clapboard sliding down toward the stone foundation whose concrete melted long ago in snow and heat, snow and heat. Decay. Swish through the timothy down the hill toward the woods ahead bobbing with the rhythm of walking. Beyond the woods, more woods, dark rounded humps vanishing into the bluish haze. The Chimp. Early in the summer he dragged a dead cow by a back leg over the rocky, dry soil, and it rotted there, melted in the sun into a lake of maggots, and the smell went all the way to town. Hey, what's that stink? I don't know.

Turn. The house roof sags, rusted corrugated sheeting, window frames bending away from square, porch posts leaning away from plumb. Decay. Beyond the house the barn and stalls. Every year The Chimp buys a piglet and raises it nine months and every year he cuts its throat in June and takes it to Mr. Evans to cut up and in a week you look at a cooked rib and remember. That you ran in the grass with the piglet, sweet-smelling and fast, who saw you and said hello with a heh heh heh heh heh low in his throat. That when it was two hundred pounds, you stood at the pen and it said heh heh heh and you said you don't know nothin' about your throat bein' cut. You don't know nothin' and I don't know nothin' and he don't know nothin' and on it goes, maggots and slit throats, summer into summer.

Deanna Branch. Just past the spring in the looming pine-needle floored woods by the red house.

The first time. Walking toward the fence past the red house and there the dense blue of jacket and a white face. A smirk. Oooo, The Chimp's kid. "What you doin' here?"

Red faced. "Uh, just walkin'."

"Walkin' where?"

"Nowhere. Just walkin' is all it is."

The second time. "Hey, what you got with this place?"

"Nothin'. I was just here lookin' at the old house. Gonna rebuild it." First time that idea ever came. "Gonna get me roofing, two-by-fours, all that."

"Really?"

Third time. Hotter and she was in the woods wearing a T-shirt and shorts. Sneakers, red puffballs above her heels. "Hey, it's you again. Where's your hammer?" When she moved the breasts rolled inside there. When she turned her breasts paused a split second before following her. Deanna Branch.

Walking. Jounce, jounce, jounce, flesh bouncing in gravity. Down the hill to the log road that vanishes into the trees, a dark tunnel lit at the opening by floating dust. Like a mine entrance. The leafed tube leading to the red house. Grandaddy Chimp dead a long time. Decayed in the cemetery. Brothers too, not dead but gone fourteen years, gone without saying anything into the service and no letters or phone calls since. Can't write letters anyway. Chimp's kids can't read like The Chimp and Mrs. Chimp can't read. Brothers gone fourteen years and the afterthought walking toward the leafed tunnel. Only strange dreamlike figures, looming above when you were two. But why? Because Jimmy has a scar on his leg from the thrust of a pitchfork when he was twelve, because Ricky has a misshapen nose from The Chimp's fist when he was thirteen. Never saw that though. Kids at school knew. Because they are covered with scars from beatings, from being The Chimp's kids.

The Chimp. Why? Because he is bowlegged and stocky and short and has long, hairy arms. Because he has a long, drooping face with a big lower lip. Because he slaps the shit out of anyone who drops anything. Because when he is mad he pinches the side, so that you are caught in a nightmare of pain. Because he can't read, never could. Because he can't write a check, never could. Because he hates any kid in his house to read or go to school, even though when he takes his papers to the village to Mr. Steele the postmaster for Mr. Steele to do all his paperwork and taxes, his long, drooping chimp face has on it a look of simpering helpless want, well, here I am again and by Jesus I can't figure this out, never could, and Mr. Steele says aww, it ain't no trouble for me, Bob. Because even when he watches TV and words come on the screen, you better not practice like you did by reading them out loud, so you mouth them softly to yourself: Just do it. Don't try this with any plugged-in razor. Buy now interest free with low monthly payments. Speeds clocked on test track only. Third and 11.

Into the tunnel. Cool, tree-smelling with shafts of dusty light slanting to the rotted leaves. Just a few hundred yards, the bubbling spring with the lump of water in the middle quickly changing shape with the upward current a little like the fountain in the hall at school. The water cold, and another fifty yards the red house. Not red now, red fifty years ago but decayed now, perforated, clapboards sliding like the woodshed, sheetmetal roofing full of holes through which thin spears of light come, dotting the rotted floor and the rusted stove.

Weeks after the cow was dragged back there and the bloat was gone, the skin draped over the bones, the maggots glistening around the edges. A week later a lake of them. And up behind the barn the faint stain of the pig's blood. Heh heh heh.

The spring, just off the logroad hidden down in the dead leaves, tiny cliffs of green moss at the edges, a cone of clear water with the lump dancing in the middle. On knees and up it sweeps, dip, and drink, the cold metallic water colder than at school.

Hate school, love school

Hate it for the smell of manure and turned milk and gasoline and pinesap in the clothes, the girls and boys sniffing insults behind the back. Hate it for the nurse who finds ticks in the scalp, nits in the hair, who puts Gentian Violet on impetigo so it is worn like a purple badge on the cheek. Hate it for the sound of their voices: hoo-hoo-hoo-hoo-haaah! and the monkey scratch of the ribs.

Love it for the books: in the quiet study hall words words words. *National Geographic. Vertebrate Paleontology. Life Beneath the Sea.* Best the big dictionary. Precarious is an old silo about to tip over. Precarious is The Chimp on the tractor on a side hill turning up so that one huge wheel leaves the ground for a split second. Unblemished is Deanna Branch's face. Unblemished is the lump of water dancing in the little conical pool. Words.

And The Chimp: you'll quit when you're sixteen because I say so. You'll quit because I need the help and that's all there is to it. You'll quit.

Oh yes the help. In May, Brownie had a shit-sodden tail and you tied it by its long, wet end-hair to a pipe beam so you could milk her, the cow who couldn't be milked by machine, and then you turned her out and she walked away from her tail in the sound of a metallic bong leaving it hanging tied there, dark empty skin, the cow walking out with a thin red stick for a tail, slick and sharp at the end. And the beating went on for five minutes (I forgot! I forgot!), strap, fist, some with a little piece of two-by-four (I forgot!), a kick in the ribs that still leaves a shadow all this time, bloody nose and hair pulled out. Oh yes the help.

No more school.  Nothing.  Only a medical book out of the dumpster behind the bus garage that last day, hidden now in the red house because The Chimp won't have it.  *The Family Medical Guide.*  Waste of time.  A lot of goddam idling.  Cutaways of human bodies and pictures of acne and clubfoot and rickets (The Chimp, probably) and uteruses and vaginas and penises and livers and spinal columns and hearts.  Pictures of different kinds of decay: rheumatoid arthritis and cancer and something of the liver.  Uh-oh, the body's precarious health.  How many thousands of miles of veins and arteries?  How many crucial organs floating in that tissue?  The heart, auricles and ventricles and valves and arteries as thick as garden hoses.  Even The Chimp has them.  Blood goes from the auricle to the ventricle.  Words.

Only fifty yards up through the trees, the red house, the tangled brush surrounding the foundation, the overgrown roses and burdocks, the faint impressions near the front where wagons once sat.  Inside the house, rotted furniture on the sagging floor, kitchen things, and in a bedroom or maybe some kind of pantry a box and inside the box the medical guide.  A kind of flutter in the chest.  Words.  *Peritonitis.  Plasma.  Pelvis.  Duodenum.  Dilation.  Deltoid.*

Deanna Branch.  As many miles of veins and arteries as the body of The Chimp's kid.  A uterus and mammary glands, a heart with four chambers, a stomach leading to a small intestine and after that to a large intestine, the whole thing a slick, glistening twenty-four feet long.  Suppose you stretched one human out that way?  All the miles of veins and arteries, and the digestive system stretched out in a line so that you could walk along it and see the protective membrane, the surrounding veins, globules of fat. Lay one out, teeth lined up, eyes sitting side by side, jawbone here, one ear on one side and one on the other, between which lies the complicated little chambered system that affects balance. The semicircular canal.

Renal failure.

Up ahead the red house. Emerging with the jouncing rhythm of walking it leans, doorway still straight while the corner beams up and down are off plumb so that clapboard has popped loose and fallen, hinged at the doorway and pointing just a little down toward the corner. A house from a dream. Big hewn granite stones for steps leading to the front door, as level as pools of water.

Stop. Listen. Deanna Branch. Only birds, a jay, in the distance the swish swish of a deer scraping past brush, groaning, breathing trees, and the soft hushed breeze in the treetops.

The red house. Those boards, gray and mossy on the bottom edges, were once red, because in the little cracks you can see it, the paint faded into a dull salmon, and then if you pull a board a little away from the doorframe, you can see the red inside, as if painted yesterday.

The house pauses in a hush like a breath held. There are clicking sounds, sounds of wood fibers sliding against each other in a slow, painful groan. The floor seems to inflate as it begins to rise, as if the basement were a huge lung gradually drawing air. The clapboards, all still and at their years of angles, shudder and just visibly begin to close up like closing scissors, the pivots where nails still hold popping and snapping as the gray wood moves. Window frames shriek as the heavy beams move slowly toward plumb, above which corrugated steel pings, surface shimmering like gasoline on water, the rust drawing inward toward its origin, closing up in a galvanized advance, the sheets sliding back into place at the edges, snaking into line and silvering in the sunlight, the blotches of rust that were nails receding into themselves revealing the perfect circles of nailheads, and as the clapboards line in, their seams go narrow until they become black lines from which the oxidized salmon of ancient paint creeps outward, brightening, advancing across the newing wood like a rapid virus, reddening and growing brighter. Brush grows backwards, shrinking into infancy and revealing windows that creep up like inverted sheets of falling water, beyond which, just visible inside, a rug spreads like a growing viral blotch on the floor that oozes gray to brown, the stain and varnish materializing like a photograph emerging out of a chemical solution, centered by the rug of brightening geometric shapes, and flowers.

"I'll get me a saw and hammer, nails, that kind of shit."

What is today? *Renal failure.* Reach through the open window to the box, topped with faded oilcloth. In the list of tiny words in the back. What is a *renal?* Read read read. A word is either one thing, or can mean something you can't touch, not a thing but a _____. Precarious.

But Deanna Branch. Page sixty-six. "Development of the breast: Left, rudimentary ducts in infancy and childhood; Center, elongation of ducts and tissue growth; Right, adult breast with milk-secreting lobules." *Lobule.*

Shirt hit by something. Burdock. Away thirty feet she stands smiling. "Hey, what you readin'?"

"Nothin'." Put it away and slide off toward the corner of the house. She comes up. Jeans, a halter. Adult breast with milk-secreting lobules.

Pull the burdock off. "Each little spike has a hook on the end. You ever see that?"

"L'me see," she says.  Hand the burdock to her.

Studies it, squinting.  "Yeah, I see them.  Neat."

Stoops and pulls a pack of Marlboros from her sock. "I come here to smoke.  So far away not even the dog smells it."

"The tar is no good for you."

"Shove it," and she giggles.  "Brought you something else too."  Digs in her jeans pocket.  Nails.  A handful of them.  Holds the nails out, drops them into your hand.

"Hey, thanks."  Hot nails.  From the heat of her tissue, the hot tissue of her thigh.

"Where's the hammer?"

"I ain't got it yet."  Put the hot nails on a gray window-sill.

Lights the cigarette with a paper match, slides the book back into the cellophane, puts the pack back in her sock. The first big puff inflates her chest, smoke billows from her mouth and nose.  "So what you like on TV?"

"Nothin'.  My dad's always watchin' cowboy movies and wrestlin'."  And he doesn't let anyone touch his little remote device.  Nobody.  Knows only a couple of the buttons but won't let anyone touch it.  Channel up, channel down, off, on.  Of menu and setup and res/mem and prog and clear he knows nothing.

"I like Beverly Hills."

"Who's she?"

Laughs so hard that she begins to cough, the veins in her neck bulging, breasts shaking.

"What's so funny?"  Face hot, scalp prickling.

"It's a place, not a girl."

"Oh."

Down below the fully developed uterus, ovaries and fal-lopian tubes rest inside the pelvic bones, all encased in skin and denim.  No congenital malformations.  A generally healthy development including the widening of the pelvis. More smoke. Every vein and every capillary now constricting, reducing body heat, especially in the extremities.

"I like to read."

Laughs again. Then, "No no no. I'm not teasing. It's just that like, like you say the weirdest things."

"I was just sayin' that because I don't watch a lot of TV. I like words so I read, anything, I don't care."

"Well, that's good."

"I want to read every book ever written."

"In English you mean. But there's like millions of them. I mean," and a gesture at the trees. "Like—" Smokes, looking.

Red face again, scalp prickling.

Words coming through smoke, "Kids at school make fun of you." So? Kids at school made fun of all of us. We're trash.

Why here? That feeling of not caring. So just say it.

"I'm The Chimp's kid."

Funny look. Turns, walks a little along the gray, decaying wood, looks in a window. "There's a real sort of new looking enamel pot in there."

"We don't have real washin' machines and stuff. So my clothes smell like woodsmoke an' cowshit."

Now a funnier look. Like she made a mistake by being— what is the word? Frank. Frank is a name and frank is a way of talking and franking has something to do with stamps.

"I could wash some of your clothes."

"Your ol' man wouldn't care for that. 'Hey what is this Chimp clothes doin' in the washer?'"

"He wouldn't say that."

Then it's up a sapling, ten, twelve feet, then higher until it bends like a fishing rod, and hanging, yell, "Hoo-hoo-

hoo-hoo-haah!" so that the sound vanishes into the woods while she seems to watch it vanish, and hanging by one arm scratch the ribs, and drop the ten feet shhh-thump in the leaves. Laugh.

"You make fun of yourself." Sits, looking. Puts the cigarette out in the wet, mulchy soil under the leaves, grinds it with the heel of her sneaker. "I never made fun of you."

"Nobody in my family could read."

"Like, what's that got to do with—"

"So I like to read. I'm gonna fix up this house and fill it with books." First time that idea ever came.

Looks. "I've got books too. You want some?"

"All you can spare. And paint it red. Was red once."

And fill it with books. Almost like a feeling of shock. Undecay it and fill it with books. Oh Jesus what an idea.

Her arms folded around her knees, the largest joints in her body. Cornered again because of that look on her face.

"What?"

"I was thinking. I could help you sort of, you know, like with the house. An old house like this, I'd bet it has a good frame still."

"This house has good bones."


Bruise expanding outward from the eye socket. Study it, the reddishness in the eye-white, a little scrape where The Chimp's fist hit. Then the side-pinch. You gonna be late again? No. You sure? Yeah, I'm sure. Cause if you are I'll beat the shit outta you. I won't be late. Damn fool, go to the woods without a gun—what the hell you do out there? Walk around is all—walking is all it is. But this time something hangs like smoke around the whole thing, around the picture of The Chimp swinging and then the sickening, silver flash of sudden pressure in the sinuses and the dizziness. Are you really allowed to do that? Or is there some other shadow of something hanging around all this and all she can say is don't be late for stuff, you know how he gets. But how he gets is still the question, if you are caught where you are and Ricky and Jimmy were caught where they were and the pigs were caught year by year and the sun went up and went down and that was all it was. Nobody knows nothin'.

Why does black paint on the back of a mirror make it silver on the other side? Not silver, it's—reflective. Some paint fell off and you can see through a hazy hole.

A bruise is a contusion caused by blows or falls that break small vessels under the skin without breaking the surface. Discoloration is temporary.

Up to the barn, into the smell of watery summer ma-nure and hay and the molasses smell of grain, the smell of wood and milk and sweaty cowhide. All up in the pasture now, only an hour ago the breathing and soft stomping on cement and the hiss chuck hiss chuck of the machines and the looks on their faces when you dumped the grain down in front of their wet, slick noses, their eyes all misty with pleasure from the molasses taste of the grain, deep pools like wells their eyes, as if you could look inside and see space itself. And an hour from now after the scrape scrape of shoveling the watery, maggot-speckled manure into the shit-spreader and washing the pails and machines scrape scrape with the wad of bright coiled steel, the red house.

Running down the hill toward the woods. Wind press-ing the eyes, heart high in the chest, the feet hardly on the ground at all. Thump thump thump, speed increasing as if you fly, the dead timothy and bright rocks and the woods ahead a blur, a jouncing smear of color.

And swoosh into the tunnel, all the way up the log road past the shimmering spring to the clearing bouncing in the distance and up then to the red house and there she sits, books on her knees.

"Hey, I brought you these. What happened to your eye?"

No breath. "How...what...uh, door."

Slamming auricles and ventricles. Eyes running— produced by the lacrimal apparatus. "I'm a little, uh, lachrymose."

Sitting. Her ball-and-socket joints permit that flexibility and range of motion, because the rounded head of the femur fits into a cup-shaped cavity in the hipbone called the acetabulum. So her thighs can be up against her chest, while the reproductive organs inside the pelvic cavity rest unblemished.

Breathe. Hold out a hand and she places the biggest on it. *American College Dictionary.* Open it to—*quarter.* "Jesus, it takes up half a page, tiny letters."

"What?"

"The word *quarter.*"

"So? A fourth, a coin, part of a football game."

"But look look look, number twenty, 'a place to stay, residence, or lodgement, esp. in military use, the buildings, houses,' and so on and so on. There are forty meanings."

"Really?"

"Where'd you get this?"

"Basement. Nobody wants it."

"I don't have anything to—hey, what's *esp?*"

"Hey, like forget it. No big deal." Cigarettes out now.

"I can't take this without—"

"Build me a nice room where I can smoke, dude."

A nice room.  The gray, sliding boards still there, the sagging floor still sagging, and if it rained, then what would happen to the dictionary, the medical book?

Another book held out, encircled by billowing smoke. Take it.   *Modern Timber Engineering*—Scofield-OBrien. Chapter I: "Structure and Characteristics of Wood. Wood differs from most other structural materials in that it is made up of cells—hollow tubes, many times as long as they are wide."

"If you like books so much, why'd you quit school?"

"My dad needs help here."

Looking up through the window past the rotted ceiling into the beams.  Then the smell of smoke.  Close, can feel the funny tangible shadow of her.

"What are you looking at?"

"Look here," pointing to page seventy-four—"Truss Types."   "That looks like a...fan truss or a king-post truss."

"You're crazy."

Close.  Can see every eyelash, the blondish down on the upper lip, the subtle pulsing of veins in the neck.  Or is it arteries?  Soft tissue surrounding the shoulder joints, which are really three separate joints acting together, permitting the great range of flexibility of motion.

"Do you have a hammer?"  From her voice box.

"There's a broken one in there."  Pointing.  Leans over into the window and looks, her hands on the sill, profile of breasts and stomach stark against the gray wood.

"Somethin' to do.  A smoking room, I mean that's—"

You would start up above the ceiling, up in the trusses to make sure they are all right, but the house has good bones.  You would start up there.  "Okay, I'm gonna climb up there and check the trusses."  Hoo hoo hah.

Baling. Ahead pulling the baler The Chimp on the bigger tractor, eating windrow after windrow, the hay pounded into the box where the heavy knives shear it off and thunk thunk thunk it is pounded out the square chute, the knotting mechanism no good on one side. Sit there in the billowing cloud of chaff and wait until the bale is just so and tie a square knot with the twine before it fouls in the tying box, over and under same side, no granny knots or they will explode, no hesitation because even with the square knot tied too late the bales will look like amber bananas. And then it will be the slap to the head, the pinch on the side.

No red house today. No Deanna Branch the perfect specimen of muscle and bone and organs and fissures and tunnels and chambers and tubes and secretions of enzymes and oils and lobules, all together in the unblemished finishment of healthy womanhood. No king post truss, no joint A and joint B, no nails for clapboards that close up like scissors into their places while only two hundred yards away past the green amber blocks of hay the newer house sags, Mother in the kitchen walking across a sagging floor so that glasses in the cupboard tinkle and the table vibrates. While only two hundred yards away wood rots, softens, fungus and moss working inward, dry rot obscuring square corners, beetles boring holes and planting grubs in the basement beams, fingerprints of rust on the stovepipe deepening until threads of smoke ooze out like tiny snakes. Slowly it melts, clapboards opening like scissors, paint fading, beams bending downward in the basement until cracks appear and widen, and then one of them breaks, fibers opening, so that the rest open and follow.

No red house today, dude.

"You can't leave until you're eighteen."

"I didn't say I would."

"They did, so why wouldn't you?"

Look. Funny expression The Chimp has, hands still gripping the taut baling twine, the bale still poised on his knee. Then up it goes onto the wagon. Follows it, pauses with his hand on his back. "Shit." Disk problem maybe?

"I think I know how to fix the knotter."

"The shit you do."

"I watched how the other one worked. It—"

"Leave it the hell alone."

The Chimp. Has his way and that's that, dude. Leave everything the hell alone. Cut up the red house for firewood probably. First time that idea came. True though. The red house. Toast.

But you can't burn words.


Through the woods upper body rocking back and forth like a gamelegged person walking, something heavy in front of her gripped with both hands, rocking and stomping, her hair swinging under her chin back and forth. Gasping for breath. Stops. "Hey, gimme a hand with this!"

Stands there with her hands on her hips—not hips but larger outside bones of the pelvic cavity since to put your fists on your hips would mean them sliding down your thighs. Closer. A bead of sweat has left her armpit and, leaving a bright trail out of the edge of white deodorant, hovers like a shimmering diamond just above the side strap of her halter. To halt what? Fabric now so insignificant compared to the weight and substance of what is halted inside. Shorts today, revealing the long, pale thighs that vanish into the tubes of the shorts' legs, up just a little more the other stuff standing straight on in a transparent display of bilateral symmetry.  Two of each thing.  Except for all the single things in the middle.

"It's paint."

"Really?"

"Red, like you said.  Barn paint.  My dad said take it, it's getting so old the can'll rot."

Carry it the rest of the way.  Strong, she must be, because this is five gallons almost.  Strong biceps and long muscles in the back.  From her house?  Jesus.

In the shade, sitting by the red house.  "Jeez, this is beginning to look good."

"Well, I replaced some beams inside, from old barn junk from the pile over there."  Point.  In those burdocks and weeds, in that tangle of old rose bushes, a foundation full of boards, some good.  "The book only shows examples of a flat Howe truss, but I used the picture for the end joints."

"Cool."

"Siding from the barn junk goes on top instead of that old sheeting.  Piece of cake.  Make a stovepipe outta roof sheeting."

Misty, distant look.  "You know, I looked it up.  There isn't a restaurant within twenty miles of here."

"Really?  Isn't the cafeteria a kind of restaurant?"

"No.  We're like in the middle of nowheresville."

"Isn't the hotel bar in town a restaurant?"

"It's a flophouse for old drunks is what it is.  I never realized—"  Hugs the knees, her chin propped, so that her head moves with each word.  "We're out of it.  Here I am sitting here by this old red house...Jesus, now even I'm seeing it red when it isn't."  Stands up now, hands on pelvic bones. "Don't you want to go someplace? I mean far away? Those girls at school, they go where they want, they rent videos, they—"

Stops. Where? Or why? "I want—" like a funny swirl of something in the head, a circling, a sweeping cyclone-like movement inward toward, "what it is, is that we're in the middle of decay." Sits again, squints. "I mean, we're at the bottom of a V of decay and now we're going to undecay." First time that idea ever came.

"I think you went right past me there, dude."

"That's why this house is going to sort of go backward away from it."

"But what do you want?"

"Nothin'. Only to see the"—Jesus, again like something clarifying in the air, something moving in the head, feeling the brain—"the design of things, that's what it is. See inside things. A truss, a knotter on a baler, the human body." Another one, Jesus. That is it, the design of things.

Looking down, sort of into her halter almost, down at her lap. "Uh-oh." Laughs.

Redfaced. Caught. The idea that she sees the idea is awful, like nakedness. "Did you know that a pillar of bone is stronger than reinforced concrete?"

A shake of the head, that funny look as if she is examining the tiny movement of chemicals through the various wires and tubes of your brain. Awful, like nakedness.

"Girls' bodies too I bet."

"Lighter and more flexible too. Bones I mean."

"Like, oh my god!" in a squeak. "Hey, which room is mine?"

Step to the window. Her breath behind, the sort of electrical field of her substance tickling your back. Of

bone and muscle, body heat, and the aroma of her, somewhere between sweat and apples.  "Right here I think,"
pointing inside.  The best room.

"Cool."

"You can smoke in there, read—"

A hand on your side— "Oops."  Almost fell.  The buzz
of the contact of hand on side—still there.

"Watch out for nails."

Looks down at the dead leaves.  "Sure thing, dude."


A tattoo of sensation, the handprint on the side, and
all through the milking and then sitting there in the dark
living room while The Chimp watches wrestling and
up-downs channels, you wait for words to come on the
screen like you used to—use as directed with diet plan,
individual weight loss may vary, world television premiere,
handcrafted pottery bowl with chopsticks—the handprint
a strange good burning on the side, as if it would be
visible there, a little redder than the skin outside it, the
touch of her flesh against his flesh, the result an oozing of
that touch down below making a boner that just won't go
away until you make it go away later in the dark when they
won't hear, when the cows and birds and insects won't
hear.  The tattoo of Deanna Branch, who in a frontal
transparency has what looks like a funny tree in her stomach, the ovaries out and hanging off single branches.


Sit and watch her, scrape scrape scrape on the pot
while under your hand the carburetor stain blotches the
tablecloth.  Mother.  Once a long-tailed pollywog called a
sperm bit its way into one of her eggs and out you came

covered with a cheesy material called vernix, out you came knowing nothing. Just do it. Funny prickling of fear.

"Ma, I'm tired of gettin' beat up for nothin'."

"Don't drop stuff." Turns from the sink and rubs her hands on the two gray spots on her apron.

"It's like he's tryin' to make me leave when I'm eighteen."

Stares, like the peculiar, precarious beginning of an idea mosquitoes around her ear. "He don' mean no real harm."

"A pitchfork is harm."

"Who tol' you that?"

"Everybody knows."

"The shit they do."

Funny, open look, like she's thinking now.

"I'm fixin' up the red house and putting books inside."

"What red house?"

"Grampa's."

"Don't you go gettin' ideas. He'll—"

"Ideas is what I'm getting. I read. I read like crazy."

"If he finds out—"

"He will. That's my place. Tell him I won't leave when I'm eighteen if he leaves it alone. Tell him I won't leave if he lets me show him how to fix the carburetor for the Ford. Tell him I'm gonna fix the knotter on the baler or at least show him how. Tell him if he punches me again, I'll stand outside the house and read a book at the top of my lungs night and day until he goes nuts. Tell him that. Tell him I'm finished being The Chimp's kid."

"You watch your mouth."

"You gonna tell him?"

Nothing. Looking as if what is sitting at the table is a thing from another planet, almost scared she looks, as if she has to watch her back because the thing is going to put a knife in it when she isn't looking.  Or knock her over the head with a dictionary.


To the woods, the red house, Deanna Branch if she isn't already in school, running down the hill with the soaring feeling of it—it's out of the bag now, you're in trouble now, dude, he's gonna kill you, but it's out of the bag now with the soaring feeling to the red house, the woods.  Stand outside and read at the top of your lungs until he goes out of his mind.  Mouth words to the TV—2.9 APR no dealer markup, make brass shine like new, coming soon to a theater near you—mouth words so loud that he'll learn them too whether he wants to or not.

In the bouncing, shifting plane of vision it comes into view, the corner nearest red almost above the window, the planking form the barn tight as anything on the beams of the roof with the king post trusses.

Out of breath.  Deanna Branch, nope.

Shit.

So more paint then.  Least if the brush isn't so goddam hard that it'd be more like a pancake flipper.  What word is that?  Spatula.  Hoo-hah!

And bingo, even before the can is open, up she comes, same shorts and halter for her mammary glands with their milk-secreting lobules.

"Know how I knew you were here?"

"No."

"I heard you crashin' through the woods like a bull."

"I told my ma this house is mine.  Hey, when do you go back to school?"

"Week."

"Hell, we'll be finished by then."

"I don't wanna go back.  Makes me wanna walk outta my skin, dude."

Stop.  Everything held like a photograph for a split second.  The skin lies in a heavy pile on the ground, the largest organ of the body, and there she stands, glistening red, musculature crisscrossed by almond-shaped muscles and thin, powerful ribbons of pale tendon, eyeballs huge in their wet sockets.

"What?"

"I...I saw you without your skin."

"Oh, that again."  Thinks.  Uh-oh, an idea of some kind.  Stares away at and idea just coming out from behind a tree.  "C'mere."

"Why?  I mean, aren't we gonna work on the house?"

Looks, hands on her hips.  "I want to show you something about the design of things."

"Wait a minute."

"When I heard you comin', I went and hid in the bushes just to see if you'd go for the medical book.  I know which pages you like 'cause the edges are all dirty.  The part about girls' bodies.  C'mere."

Hate it.  Flushed face and shaky knees.  Hate it.  Caught.  Caught doin' something dirty.  "No."

"I won't hurt you."

Like the ground tips, trees lean, the sun jerks over a little, and the swirl spirals inward and the smell of sweat and fear billows out of the shirt top like stale breath.

"At school they talk about it all the time.  The town girls, and what do I get to talk about?  How I went and picked flowers for my mom?  Changed my little sister's nasty diapers?"

"Actually, the best ideas I ever got were when I was talkin' to you."

"Okay, like here we go again. I mean like jeez Louise, what the hell does that mean?"

"I–"

"All I wanted was just to... I mean, it isn't like it's something I like plan to talk about, all right?"

"What do you want me to do?"

"C'mere is all I said."

Step, step, crunch leaves. Awful, like the time the teacher said stand at the front of the class and tell us blah blah blah. No control. The muscles just don't work.

"Give me your hand."

Laugh. What, do you unscrew it? Or does it just pop off?

"C'mon."

Takes it by the wrist with her right hand. Pull back. "C'mon, I'm not going to bite you. Jeez. Close your eyes."

Red black, sight through the lids. When the hand touches flesh there is no question, the softness and warm liquidity, the weight, the electrical current of living human tissue with the faint, precarious blipping of a rapid heartbeat. Faster than your own. The hand gripping the wrist pulls it tighter on the flesh, and the eyes open to her face staring back, mouth open, a look of experimental awe, eyes boring straight into a face with the same expression. Lifts the wrist a little, mashes the hand around in little circles, and the index finger feels the harder rounded edge of pectoral muscle, deeper down the surface of a rib. Then the wrist is released, and the hand departs slowly, the soft tissue following it until the last contact is gone. Back goes the halter.

Giggles. "Scared you? You scared?"

"Yeah." Heart slamming, even blips the vision brighter with each beat. "I mean...yeah, scared."

"It's like no big deal after all. I just wanted to show you something about, you know."

"Design."

"Can we work on the house now?"

The face so sort of normal, little hairs on the upper lip reflecting sunlight in tiny amber and golden needles. Calmer now. Raise the hand and smell it.

"What?" Laughing, shaking her hand.

"I couldn't help it."

"You smelled your hand?"

Look away, think. Nothing to think. "You ever heard of narcolepsy?" Her face held still, a mask of wonder on the edge of laughing. "Or catalepsy? How they put epsy on the ends of things?"

"Uh-oh, here we go again."


Always know by the way The Chimp sort of circles that he's getting ready to swing. The idea backs away, the idea holds up a hand and tucks the *Operator's Manual* under the arm and, "Look, all I'm sayin' is that of all the parts on the table I didn't see no float lever shaft."

"Get high and mighty with me an' I'll clean your clock."

"All I'm sayin' is that without the float lever shaft you can't put it back together."

Sneers. "You read that in there?"

"Yeah, I read it in here." Hold it out. Hey, it won't bite. "If we can't find it, we can make one out of a piece of wire or a little nail or something."

"You think you're hot shit don't you."

"No. But that isn't the problem. Listen to this—"

Circles a little, looking, that wounded anger on his

Chimp face. Oh does he hate it, does he ever hate the idea that there's an idea in front of him.

"'Engine backfires but will not start. This symptom indicates that the spark plugs are not firing in their proper order, either due to the ignition high tension system being shorted, the spark plug wires being transposed, or the camshaft out of time. Perform the following operations in the order given.' That might be the problem."

Surprise on The Chimp's face. "L'me see that."

Hand it to him.

"Where's it say that?"

Point. "Here, 'Engine backfires but will not start.' That's what that says."

"No shit."

"That's what it says."

"So what are these operations?"

"We put the carburetor back together first."

"What about that thing, that—"

"We'll make one."

The Chimp thinking. The idea of beating up on the little Chimp gone, like smoke in the wind. Thinking, churning something through the brain like food in a stomach. You don't know nothin' and then you know there's somethin' you don't know and that's where it all starts. Holds the lower lip between a dirty, grime-blackened thumb and a dirty, grime-blackened finger, pulls on it a little. "So how much more schoolin' would you hafta have to do the paper stuff, milk check and taxes and all that shit? How much more?"

"I can do it now."

"The shit you can."

"No, I can do it. You wouldn't hafta take it down to Mr. Steele. I can do it easy."

"Like shit you can."

In the red house. *The Medical Guide.* Nothing about weight, or heat. Nothing about the bright secret buzz of electricity. Nothing about the power of human tissue to scare. Nothing about the awful tickling surge of some strange, complicated system of racing liquids built into the design that squirt around every cell and tickle every organ and vein, all four chambers of the heart with its precarious blipping. Nothing about standing so close and being engulfed by the vapor of her presence, by the contact with one body part radiating inside into all the secret tubes and chambers and valves and membranes and filters and tiny assembly lines of cells.

Three-thirty has to be, the way the sun slants in through the paneless window onto the gray, dusty floor.

Dictionary—go for the page even before the idea of going for it has formed, and there it is a third of a column long.

"Don't close it."

Up from the chair, heart slamming. "Jesus."

"School sucks. You shoulda heard those girls."

Turn, heart still slamming.

"Don't touch it—I wanna see what you looked up. What girl's body part did you look up today?"

As if the heart sort of exploded right out of the chest cavity sending bits of lung and bone pinwheeling through the air and going splat, some sticking to the wall, some arcing out the open window hole to land in the leaves outside. A grenade made of tissue, blam.

"What's the matter?"

"I...you scared me."

"I got you these."

Books. Focus now, the same halter and shorts, she has changed out of her school clothes. Take the books, the hand holding them leaking electricity through the pages and covers into your own, electricity from the whole of her body, from every corner having passed through every part, having made every single hair sort of glow like a tungsten filament. *Little Women* and *Exploring Poetry*, hot from her hands.

"Thanks."

"What were you looking up?"

Move toward it and she tries to go around, laughing. Been eating mint candy, she has. It's in her breath, going in and out of her lungs and then into your nose, proof that you breathe her breath.

"By the way, *Little Women* isn't about midgets."

"Oh." And they will go in alphabetical order even though there are only five of them, all lined up neatly on the shelf like shoulder to shoulder, dictionary one side, *Modern Timber Engineering* on the other.

Nothing to do now. Caught again. Leaning over, her hands on either side of the dictionary palms down, the long muscles of her back making the valley of her spine, the denim depressing the flesh in a circle around her waist. Apples and mint, and the hushed odor of mysterious enzymes evaporating on her skin.

"It's nothin'. I was just—"

"Shh."

Finger moves down the first column and you are caught, standing at attention as if waiting to be shot, as if the next words will be hoo hah! as if she will laugh and run, something to tell the oh my gosh girls. Like would you believe what—

Finds the word love and stands up, face stilled with dumbstruck wonder, the idea exploring her brain like little hands feeling their way while she holds still feeling them, the little hands making something like a sculpture that the backs of her eyes seem to follow, to watch. Then it forms and she blinks, her mouth slowly opening in the formation of a word.

"Uh-oh."

# The Proper Axis

His father sat in the living room watching wrestling, and he waited until there was an ad and went in.

"Here's the letter," he said, holding it out.

His father looked up at him, his expression blank, then thoughtful.

"So?" He didn't reach for the letter.

"I needed a ride to the school."

"'Ride,' He says." His father turned back to the TV. "Gotta milk," he said to it. "You too."

"Jimmy can do my share. I'll make it up."

It was four o'clock, and clear now that if he were going, he had to walk or hitch. The awards ceremony was at seven. He was fairly sure about the award he was getting, for a high score in a typing Regents Test, and the idea of it embarrassed him. He had taken a lot of ragging about it from his friends, all hill people who found the idea of an academic award so stupid that they could easily laugh themselves silly over it.

"So it's probably only for typing," he told them. "I mean, gimme a break. Typing is all it is."

"Hey, Glenn, you gonna get a job as a 'thecretary'?"

Standing there watching his father as the wrestlers appeared again, he snorted and muttered, "The hell with it," and stuck the letter in his back pocket. He took off his glasses and cleaned them with the hem of his shirt. Then he went to the kitchen where his younger brother, who had already quit school, was sitting before a dismantled carburetor spread out on the sticky plastic table cloth.

His mother stood at the sink.

"Hey, cover for me tonight," he said.

"'Cover,' he says," Jimmy repeated. "Up yours, Glenn."

"Hey," their mother said, turning from the sink.

"I'll give you part of my award."

"How do you know it's money?"

"It's always money. I'll give you five bucks."

Jimmy snorted. "Ten."

"Seven."

"S'pose the award is five bucks?"

"Then you'll get half of it."

"You'll owe me two bucks. How you gonna get there?"

"Fly."

"It's twelve miles."

"Eight crosslots. I'll check the traps on the way."

Jimmy snorted, and their mother turned back to the sink.

"I ain't seen a muskrat since Mickey Mouse died," Jimmy said. "Pelts ain't worth anything, anyway. Forget it. I took 'em all in."

"Crosslots means deer ticks," his mother said, without turning from the sink. "You can't—"

"Yes, I can," he said. "I can see a grain of pepper."

"Grain of pepper with legs," Jimmy said, hunching over the carburetor parts.

"I can see," Glenn said. "Not afraid of deer ticks anyway. There probably aren't any here."

His eyes had been bad all his life—severe astigmatism. The school had offered free exams when he was fifteen, and he had looked into the lenses of a machine that showed numbers against a bright background while the optometrist talked about horizontal and vertical images, about drawing the axis of these images together. He recommended to Glenn's parents that they buy glasses for him, or contact lenses. His father refused, until the optometrist lowered the price for glasses to within a range he had to accept, even though it was grudgingly. Glenn's mother convinced him, mostly. Contacts were too expensive. Glenn could tell, even without being able to see clearly, how angry his father was at having to pay for them. Like all of the families in the area, Glenn's had no money.

"So, how about maybe a ride to the hard road?" he asked. No one answered. That would cut four miles off, and he could hitch the rest of the way. Jimmy kept working on the carburetor. "Well," Glenn said, "I'll go then."

"What's the biggest prize they give?" Jimmy asked.

"I don't know."

"Hundred? If you get that, then you can buy a gun, a thirty-ought-six. I'll go for that."

"I don't know."

"Well, that's what you said. You said you were going to blow away chucks and birds. That's what you told everybody."

He had said that to his friends at school, before he got the glasses, had dreamed of the day when he could hit a chuck at a hundred yards. "I don't know," he said, and went out the back door.

He walked across the dirt road and over the large pasture to the woods, on a path he had been taking since he got his glasses. It would go through their woods, past the rotted remains of his grandfather's house to the Hoags' woods and then to the hard road. His father had been in a spat with the Hoags for years over the property line, and had cut logs as he saw fit, even if he wasn't sure he was on his own property. The last time it was an ash tree, and Hoag got so mad that he drove around to their driveway and yelled at the house that the next time he saw anybody cutting wood there he'd blow their brains out. Glenn had stood at the window, staring wide-eyed at the man's expression as he yelled, the red, sweaty face through the glasses bright with a pinpoint lucidity. Later he tried to explain the problem to his father. "You gotta understand that an ash tree is valuable—"

"Shut up," his father said. "I do what I want."

For Glenn these woods lay in his perception as two distinct entities. One, before the glasses, was an environment of bright, fuzzy colors where he would see a deer, a brown, amoebic shape inside the snorting and thudding of hooves in the dead leaves, and the swishing of hide against brush. Or birds, amorphous shapes flashing across the muddied plane of colors. He understood later that he had accepted the way he saw things. The only things he could see fairly clearly were close up, where the distortion was minimized. He had grown up reading, and whenever his father caught him doing that, he would say, "Cut that out. You'll only make them worse." His mother seemed to like the idea of his reading and told him that the grandparents were readers.

And then he got the glasses. The optometrist had placed them on his face, and he had turned and looked out through a door and had been made dizzy with shock at the sharpness of what he saw. A young woman, an attendant or some sort of nurse, came in holding a case for him, and he became so frightened at the lucidity of what he saw that he stumbled backwards as if blinded: a pretty face, eyes framed top and bottom by hundreds of curved lashes, a tiny scar on her forehead, fine amber hairs on her upper lip and cheeks, and the top button of her blouse open enough for him to see three tan freckles on her chest. It was as if she had walked into the room naked.

As he walked through the woods he pictured the school and felt a swoon of embarrassment wash over him. Ahead the sun came through the treetops in shafts in which dust moved, so they looked like tipped, silver pillars. At school the glasses made for a change that shamed him. From the first day, he became obsessed by the clarity of his vision, to the point that, without knowing it, he did things that made his friends and his brother look at him with a kind of skeptical impatience. When he first saw birds clearly, he took a bird identification book out of the library and carried it with him. Still amazed at how he could identify things, he showed a picture to one of his friends at school. "A scarlet tanager, they call it. See?" and he pointed to the picture. His friend stared at him blankly, then said, "Gee, that's thweet."

His grandfather's house sat in a tangle of brush in a partial clearing, old rose bushes obscuring the fieldstone foundation. As he approached it, he studied the old boards and the perforated corrugated steel roof, which sent shafts of light into the weed-choked interior. Inside there was rotted furniture, rusty bed frames, books fused together by rot, broken dishes and lamp chimneys, rusted tools, and little things like toothless combs, a broken briar pipe, and corrosion-softened silver tops from salt and pepper shakers. A porcupine lived under the living room floor. When he was able to see all these things, he again became caught by the idea of understanding them, and studied the few old photographs of that house that his mother kept in a drawer. He found his grandmother's rocking chair, some of the dishes, and his grandfather's pipe.

In English class he wrote a paper about the house, describing the condition of what was left of it, and the porcupine, whose bristly back he had seen, the white needles in ranks against dark fur, when he moved a floorboard to figure out what had made a sound. The teacher made him read it to the class, which was so mortifying that he barely heard her when she said, "There's no title, Glenn," to which he replied, "Title?" She laughed and said, "Okay, I'll give it one."

His friends would not let him forget what the teacher called his "sensitivity" to what he saw. They made retching sounds whenever the subject came up, ragged him mercilessly when they drank beer and smoked cigarettes in their old cars after school. And his only defense was to go along with them, saying in a high, prissy voice, "Oh dear, my grandmother's rocker! How awful!" and then he would lapse into a girlish sobbing while they cackled with laughter.

Behind the wreckage of the house he heard the sound of someone trying to start a chainsaw, the repeated hollow five-beat surge of the piston failing to blow. Hoags. He decided to work his way a little south of them so as to avoid being seen. He checked the sun, realized that he had plenty of time, even enough to poke around the old house if he wanted to. Then he paused, thinking that this was pretty stupid for the fifteen or twenty bucks he'd get. Back at the barn they'd already be milking; he decided to go on, picturing himself accepting the check amid the jeers and snickers of friends whose parents forced them to go.

He could not explain to them how he felt about the sight they all took for granted. He could not explain to them how frightened he was when he was putting a milking machine on a cow and her whipping tail knocked his glasses off into the gutter filled with dark green, watery summer manure shimmering with maggots. He had plunged his hands into the soup to the sound of his brother's laughing and then stumbled, breathless and almost sobbing, out the barn doorway to the water vat to clean them. He remained horribly frightened until he was finally able to put them back on.

He could not explain to his brother, who loved shooting birds with his .22, what it felt like in spring to walk through the woods with the chickadees following him, each one so close that he could see every minute detail of eyes and feathers and toothpick-thin legs. He could not explain how he felt that day when he walked along a gully one late winter morning and saw a buck, twenty feet away, standing there steaming in the bright morning sunlight, the breath vapor shooting from its snout and the steam leaving his back like tongues of white fire. In an English class essay about these walks he had tried to describe these things but felt that words could not stand one hundred percent for vision. In fact, he made that the point of the essay. Mercifully, the teacher didn't make him read that one, although she gave it an "A."

"Well lookee here."

He turned. Mr. Hoag stood thirty feet away, his son Lonnie by his side. They were very clear, intense in color,

Lonnie's face crossed with a look of good-humored chal-
lenge.

"I'm just goin' to the school awards thing," Glenn
said.

"I told you not to set foot here," Mr. Hoag said. "I'll
fill your ass with buckshot."

"Look," Glenn said, "if it was up to me I'd give you the
ash tree back."

"'Give the ash tree back,' he says," Mr. Hoag said to
Lonnie, who snorted.

"No, I mean I understand," Glenn said. "I mean, I
like—tried to explain to him, but he—"

"You don't understand nothin', four-eyes," Hoag said.
"He's been cutting here so long that—"

"No, I understand how you'd be like, like mad and all,
that's all I was saying. I tried to tell him."

"Well, ain't that nice," Hoag said. Then to his son:
"That's nice, ain't it?"

"It sure is," Lonnie said. "I mean, Jesus!"

"I'm just goin' on to the hard road. Go back, if you
want."

"G'wan," Hoag said.

Glenn turned to go back.

"No, g'wan to the hard road. What you getting?"

"Some award for typing."

"Typing?" Hoag said, and scowled to his son. "For
typing what?"

"A Regents test score, is all."

"Regents test," Hoag said, and then to his son, "You
ever taken one of those Regents tests?"

"Not that I remember," Lonnie said, and laughed.
"Let's see—Regents test. Nope, never have."

The hard road, black macadam that snaked through
the hills like a huge strip of frayed black electrical tape,

was empty both ways. When Glenn stooped through the barbed wire he was careful not to catch his shirt or his jeans, and realized he was not really dressed right for the ceremony. But, what the hell, he thought. You collect your money and you leave. He figured it was five-thirty. He walked along on the wrong side of the road for hitching because he had plenty of time.

As he walked, cars passed along on the way to town, cars came the other way, people waved. A group of friends came from town and shuddered to a halt.

"Where you goin'?" one yelled.

"Hey, Billy," Glenn said. "School. The awards thing."

"We're goin' to my place—beer, then coon huntin'. Whatcha think?"

"Nah, I gotta go to this awards thing."

They sped off, and he watched, wishing he'd gone with them. He didn't know why, but the glasses had created a strange distance between him and them, and he didn't like the feeling.

The auditorium was full when he got there, sweeping away from him like a carpet of heads. The brown and blonde blended with gray to form a rich variety which, when he squinted and briefly removed his glasses, became a deep tan. He stood in the back, not wanting to climb over people to get to the single seats he saw available. His clothes had a slight manure and turned milk smell, and he didn't like close proximity to other people. Because he was tired from the walking, the sound dimmed and became tinny and hollow.

He found a chair and placed it against the wall to the left of the last row, and as they called one after another student up—science award, Honors award, scholar-athlete award—he sneaked glances at a girl named Laura Shipman, from his class, sitting with her parents in the seats nearest him. He studied her profile, her hands holding a rolled up program, her feet crossing, uncrossing, until she seemed to become aware of him and he stopped. He had trouble controlling the impulse because, even after almost two years, vision itself seemed to him as fresh and valuable as during those first days.

He took his glasses off and saw his old vision, and felt an involuntary surge of fear at the idea of losing them. Once, after getting the glasses, he looked in an art book in study hall and turned to what was called an impressionistic street scene, which made him shudder, because of its vague, cottony lack of definition. For him it was no more than an astigmatic street scene.

His name was called for what Mr. Wenkham, the principal, called the John Everett Shields Award, and as he walked down the aisle, feeling strange about his clothes, Mr. Wenkham explained that it was for an essay titled "The Porcupine's House," submitted to a statewide competition by his English teacher.

He became muddled and unsure, walking up the three steps, and went and took the envelope, shook Mr. Wenkham's hand, and then went off the stage. "That prize, by the way, is $350," he said, and Glenn kept walking, staring at the dirty strip of floral rug under him, back to his seat, to the sound of applause and a couple of shrill whistles. He peeked in the envelope at the check, then sat through the rest of the awards clutching the envelope. There was no award for typing.

He got out before the rest of them and walked through the town in the dark, then out toward home, against traffic, of which there was little since the hill types rarely went to these meetings. As he walked he calculated—three-hundred-and-fifty-dollars, thirty or more cases of beer, three hundred-and-fifty-dollars, a 30-06, three-fifty, God-knows-how-long a supply of cigarettes, three-fifty—

When he was about five miles out of town, a car stopped. It was Mike Stringer, a farmer who lived only a mile down the road. "Hey, boy, it's after ten, for chrissakes. Hop in." He took Glenn home and, walking up the long driveway, Glenn saw that all the lights were out. Everyone had to get up at five.

In the kitchen the next morning, he explained to his parents what the award was for, and he saw on his father's face a strange look, a blank disbelief that melted into the appearance of irritated greed. "I understand," Glenn said. "Look, I'll cash this and give you a hundred and fifty, but I want to—"

"You don't gotta," his father said. But the look was still there.

"No, I'll just give you the hundred and fifty. I mean, you paid the sixty for the glasses, but I want to—" He wasn't sure what he was saying, and he felt guilty for not giving him more.

And in the barn he explained the award to his brother, who jumped up from a milking machine, leaving the four stainless steel cups on the ends of red rubber hoses dangling under a cow. "Jesus, you can get a 30-06, even one of those surplus high-powers—and Enfield .303. None of that peashooter stuff."

"Well, I was thinking of those things, those other lenses. Contacts. I mean, he said I could get them for—But it was too much. But I got enough now."

His brother stared at him with an almost horrified disbelief. "Are you nuts?" he asked.

"That's what I was thinking of. Do you see—"

"Oh, that's great," his brother said, and went back to the machine. "Oh wow! That's cool." When he stood up again, above the hiss-chuck hiss-chuck of the machine, Glenn saw the grudging hatred on his face.

"I understand," he said. "I just gotta do this. If you could just see how—"

"You moron."

"There isn't anything I want to shoot right now."

"You stupid pansy moron."

Glenn turned and went to the barnyard doorway, his face hot, and then out to the water vat. He looked at the perfect surface of the water, and at the slimy sides of the interior. "I understand," he whispered. The water, coming from up the hill through a pipe, had seeped so slowly into the vat that for years it had run over the down-hill edge, creating a tiny, fan-shaped track, bright green with moss, all the way to the mud and then in the mud, a perfect, sharply cut little canyon through which the clear water trickled, leaving bright pebbles in the bottom.

an MacMillan is the author of a dozen previous books. His honors include the O. Henry Award, the Pushcart Prize, Best American Short Stories, the Associated Writing Programs Award for Short Fiction, the National Endowment for the Arts fellowship in fiction, the PEN-USA West Award, and the Hawai`i Award for Literature. After growing up in New York state where the stories in *Our People* are set, MacMillan taught at the University of Hawai`i at Mānoa for many years.